GHOST STORIES

STORIES

of

INDIANA

Edrick Thay

LONE
PINE

Lone Pine Publishing International

D0920696

The Publisher: Lone Pine Publishing International
Distributed by Lone Pine Publishing

10145 – 81 Avenue
Edmonton, AB T6E 1W9
Canada

1808 B Street NW, Suite 140
Auburn, WA 98001
USA

Website: www.lonepinepublishing.com

National Library of Canada Cataloguing in Publication Data
Thay, Edrick, 1977–
    Ghost stories of Indiana

    ISBN 13: 978-1-894877-06-0
    ISBN 10: 1-894877-06-3

3 3113 03018 1301

    1. Ghosts—Indiana. 2. Legends—Indiana. I. Title.
GR110.I6T42 2002   398.2'0977205   C2002-910700-8

Editorial Director: Nancy Foulds
Project Editor: Shelagh Kubish
Editorial: Shelagh Kubish, Denise Dykstra, Sandra Bit
Illustrations Coordinator: Carol Woo
Production Coordinator: Jennifer Fafard
Cover Design & Illustrations: Gerry Dotto, Ian Dawe
Layout and Production: Ian Dawe

Photo Credits: Every effort has been made to accurately credit photographers. Any errors or omissions should be directed to the publisher for changes in future editions. The photographs in the book are reproduced with the generous permission of their owners: © The Library of Congress (p. 20, p.109); Willard Library, Evansville, Indiana (p. 42); Skiles Test Elementary School, Indianapolis, Indiana (p. 58); University of Notre Dame Archives (p. 79, p. 82); Purdue University Library, Special Collections (p. 90, p.92); Town of Avon, Indiana (p. 127); *The Journal,* Ellettsville, Indiana (p. 153).

PC: P5

Dedication

To my family for their love and support

Acknowledgments

It's cliché to say, but without the help of so many people, there would be nothing but many blank pages following this one. The assistance of those both in Indiana and in Alberta has proven invaluable and indispensable, and I'm grateful to all who prodded me along the way.

I'd be remiss if I didn't thank those Hoosiers who provided me with the stories and reports you're holding in your hands now. Many thanks and my deepest appreciation to Ken and Mary Bowman and Robert MacDonald of the National Haunted Registry, Mark Bristow of the Sigma Pi Fraternity Headquarters, Rich Davis of the Evansville Courier, Luann Dillon of the Monroe County Public Library, Tom Moulds, Judith Nagata of Hanover College, Susie Richter of the La Porte County Historical Society, Suzanne Stanis of the Historical Landmarks Foundation, Moira L. Smith of the Folklore Institute at my alma mater, Indiana University, Wanda Lou Willis, the Francesville Public Library, the Miami County Historical Society, the New Albany Historical Society, the Vigo County Historical Society and Vincennes University. I'm indebted to websites such as <theshadowland.net/ghost/> and <rking.vinu.edu> for providing a forum for individuals to relate their personal experiences. These sites have allowed me, working in Alberta, to reach out from the heart of the Canadian prairies and feel the pulse of the American heartland. A special thank you to those of you who permitted and trusted me to tell your stories. You know who you are.

I also want to thank those who've already walked the trail down which I've just traveled, those writers, archivists and journalists who've paved the way and made my work easier and harder—easier in that their work provided me with a firm foundation on which to stand; harder in that I realized how high the bar had already been set for ghost writers in Indiana. My gratitude and respect go out to Ronald Baker, Linda Degh, Howard Dukes, Mark Marimen, K.T. MacRorie, Arthur Myers, Paul Startzman and journalists past and present at the *Bloomington Herald-Times*, the *Indianapolis Star*, the *Indiana Daily Student*, *FATE*, the *South Bend Tribune*, and other newspapers and magazines throughout the state.

Finally, I would like to express my thanks to the staff at Ghost House Books, notably Dan Asfar for providing me with comic relief during those times I was ready to heave either myself or my manuscript out the window; Shelagh Kubish and Denise Dykstra, for their able and sure editing, which has made my words sound better than ever; Carol Woo, for supplying the images without which this text would be less than what it is; Nancy Foulds for her much-needed guidance and faith in me; and Shane Kennedy for providing me with this opportunity to do that which I love best: write.

Thank you.

Contents

Chapter 5: Bridges & Transport

Chapter 6: Haunted Cemeteries

Chapter 7: Legends of Indiana

1
Haunted Houses

We like to think of our homes as secure, private places, havens where we can escape the pressures and stresses of our daily lives. Our homes are meant to be our Edens, our own little Utopias. We rarely consider in the daily comings and goings of our lives that we might very well be the snakes in other people's gardens, that we might be, even in our houses, disturbing and intruding upon the peace of another. Many houses, after all, develop a character all their own over time, displaying various elements from their own particular colored pasts. Sometimes, these elements can be found in decorative touches and architectural design. But every now and then, a building's past will reveal itself in unexpected ways. It seems that in some homes, previous inhabitants prefer not to go quietly into that good night, and instead choose to remain well past their passing. It's a living arrangement that makes for some spirited stories.

Help From Beyond

West 6th Street in Muncie, Indiana, is home to a house unlike any other. There's little in the way of architecture to set this particular dwelling apart, but the residence boasts its own spirit—a ghost that has added to one family's sense of comfort and security. An account sent to me by the family explained the history of the haunting.

In 1985, the Gasper family moved to Muncie and immediately became dismayed at the obscene amounts landlords were asking for rent. Imagine their surprise, then, when they happened to find a pleasant two-story home and a landlord offering to lease the place at half the price he'd been quoting all day long at his other properties.

No deposit or security was required, and when the Gaspers asked why, the landlord merely mentioned that tenants never stayed in this particular residence for longer than two months. The young family jumped at the opportunity, and as the place was furnished, all they had to do was unpack and begin adding those personal touches that transform a house into a home.

The children moved into the bedroom on the main floor, for the stairs of the house were steep and Mrs. Gasper didn't want one of her youngsters to wake up in the middle of the night and accidentally fall. The two bedrooms upstairs were turned into a playroom, and it was there that Mrs. Gasper and her brood spent their days whiling away time in the realms of make-believe and fantasy. Within weeks, though, the line between the natural and supernatural worlds began to blur.

Strangely, the children always avoided the south bed-room of the play area. "If there was a toy in there that they wanted, they would ask [me] to get it for them," said Mrs. Gasper. "Or they would make a mad dash into the bedroom, grab the toy and run back into the north bedroom."

Curious, Mrs. Gasper asked the kids why they avoided the room. They simply responded that they found it "scary." The oldest child, a girl of three, said that "she didn't like the old lady in the room" and that the lady "looked mean at her" if she played in there. But an old lady didn't live with the Gaspers. It suddenly became clear why tenants never stayed in the house longer than two months. The home was haunted.

The spirit did not frighten the Gaspers, though. Mrs. Gasper had been taught from a young age by her maternal grandmother "that spirits live around us, everywhere, in every home, every empty lot…existing on a different plane." She believed that "all humans are born with the ability to 'see' into this other plane but most choose to block that ability, either from fear or ignorance."

As a child, Mrs. Gasper had been encouraged to peer continually into the other plane. So she found the idea of the spirit of an old woman residing in her new home far from unusual—it was to be expected and embraced. To assuage her young child's fears, Mrs. Gasper told her simply that the old woman was mean only because she didn't know yet just how sweet the child could be.

As the days and weeks passed, routine and habit rendered the strange and the eerie familiar and comfortable. The Gaspers became accustomed to waking up, walking into the kitchen and seeing their refrigerator door wide open. It was certainly puzzling, as none of the young children had the strength to open the heavy door, but the Gaspers attributed the phenomenon to nothing other than the settling of the house. Until, that is, other things began to happen, occurrences that could not have been caused by shifts in the ground.

The family began to hear muffled noises from upstairs, usually late in the night. Mrs. Gasper likened the sound to a "kind of soft pacing back and forth across the south bedroom floor, directly in front of the window on the south wall."

When Mrs. Gasper would check on her children to make sure they were sleeping comfortably, she would find them completely tucked into their beds. Their blankets would be wedged between the mattress and its box spring, something that Mrs. Gasper never did. The kids found it odd as well, complaining that they couldn't move. All Mrs. Gasper would do was loosen the covers and, before leaving the bedroom, utter a silent thanks. "I knew someone was watching over them in their sleep," she says.

Naturally, Mrs. Gasper was curious about who was keeping an eye on her children. As time passed, she became acquainted with her neighbors, an old couple who had moved to Muncie in the early 1950s. Over morning coffees and afternoon teas, Mrs. Gasper began to ask them about her home's history.

Before long, Mrs. Gasper discovered that the house had become a rental property in the early 1970s, after its original inhabitants, an old mother and her mentally handicapped son, passed into the afterlife within two weeks of each other. Sadly, the son had become entangled in his blankets one evening—trapped like a fly in a spider's web—and smothered to death. His blankets had not been tucked in securely between the mattress and its box spring.

Mrs. Gasper discovered that the boy had died in the upstairs south bedroom. The death broke the mother's spirit and she spent the rest of her days pacing back and forth in front of the room's window. Her grandson found her dead, lying on the floor beneath the window. While coroners claimed she died of natural causes, those who knew her said she died of guilt and a broken heart.

Death may have removed the mother's and son's corporeal forms from this plane of existence, but both seemed to be alive and well on that other plane of which Mrs. Gasper's maternal grandmother spoke so fondly. Apparently, the mentally handicapped son had the habit of waking in the night and taking a jar of mayonnaise from the fridge. He refrained from shutting the door for fear of rousing his mother. Evidently the mother didn't like the idea of other kids frolicking in the room in which her son had died. Maybe the exultant cries of children at play reminded her of her tragic loss.

The Gaspers moved out of the home a year later when they relocated to the country. Until that time they never complained about their housemates. They continued to hear the pacing upstairs late at night and, on occasion, to find the fridge door wide open. And when Mrs. Gasper checked on her children and found them tightly tucked in, she continued to utter a thanks to the old mother, a spirit desperately trying to rectify the wrongs of the past.

The Gaspers were aware that while those who had lived in the house on West 6th Street would claim they were haunted by ghosts, it was actually the living that haunted the dead.

Hannah House

The Hannah House on Madison Avenue in Indianapolis is a grand example of Italianate architecture. It's also a great illustration of a home with a tragic past that is said to exert a powerful force on those who live within its walls.

The 24-room red brick mansion was built two years before the Civil War by Indiana state legislator Alexander Hannah. The house was much more than a simple residence. Hannah sympathized with the plight of slaves, and his basement was a stop on the Underground Railroad. Runaways would hide in its chambers before continuing with their journey.

One unfortunate evening, a lantern was knocked over and a fire swept through the basement. The flames were eventually extinguished, but not before countless slaves lost their lives. Hannah buried the dead in simple coffins in the room where they had perished. That way he could continue to keep his Underground Railroad station a secret.

Some time later, personal tragedy also struck the Hannah family. Hannah's wife, Elizabeth, gave birth to a stillborn baby in a second-floor bedroom. The child was buried in the Crown Hill Cemetery in the family plot, with nothing but a small, unmarked gravestone hinting at what lay beneath.

By 1899, the Hannahs were gone, and until 1962, various generations of the Oehler/Elder families lived in the house. In 1962, David Elder became the home's caretaker, but he chose to live elsewhere, perhaps disturbed by the first of the mansion's reported hauntings.

Elder had been working around the house one day when he was surprised to hear the sound of glass shattering from the basement . He went downstairs, but search as he did, he found nothing. All he could see were some fruit jars stored in the same area where Hannah had buried his lost slaves.

Elder also noticed strange odors emanating from the second-floor bedroom where Elizabeth Hannah had lost her baby. Over time, that bedroom had been converted into a storage room, which was always kept locked. Yet something or someone was finding a way in; the door would mysteriously open on its own and the smells of decaying flesh or sweet roses would flood the halls. It is said that the former was enough to make anyone gag and run for fresh air.

And then there were the sounds. People reported hearing footsteps along with muffled voices that had no visible source. It was enough to drive a painter away from his job of refinishing the rooms. He supposedly lost his nerve when he saw a spoon on a tray fly across the room.

By 1968, the Elders had left the home to its spirits, and the O'Brien family had moved in. They opened up an antique store on the first floor of the mansion. It is said that during their stay, the ghosts roaming the Hannah House truly began to make their presence known.

One night just before closing Mrs. O'Brien saw a man in a black suit wandering around the upstairs hallway. She thought little of the man, assuming that he was a customer who had mistakenly found his way to the second floor. But when she climbed the stairs to tell the customer to go back to the shop, the man in black had vanished.

Mr. O'Brien also saw the figure, this time standing under an archway on the stairs. His suit clearly marked him as a visitor from the past, but before Mr. O'Brien could inspect him more closely, the figure vanished into thin air once again.

Mr. O'Brien eventually got more than a little annoyed with the unwelcome visitor and finally confronted the apparition one evening while he was watching television upstairs. From somewhere beyond his bedroom door and down the second-floor hallway, Mr. O'Brien could hear loud groans. Rather than being terrified, the antique shop owner bellowed down the hall, commanding the ghost to stop bothering him and his wife.

Surprisingly, by 1972 the hauntings seemed to have ceased altogether. Whatever Mr. O'Brien had yelled at had obviously gotten the message. The O'Briens lived in the home for six more years, ghost-free the entire time.

It wasn't until the early 1980s that the spirit or spirits of the Hannah House reared their heads again. By this time, the mansion was being used as an annual haunted house project by the Indianapolis Jaycees. Children were given tours of the home and scared out of their wits by the effects the Jaycees would add for entertainment. Ironically, it was the Jaycees and not their little guests who reportedly became terrified.

One night, a coordinator and other workers were resting in the kitchen. The kitchen was next to the servants' staircase, and without warning loud scratching sounds were heard coming from inside the wall, as if something or someone were trying to claw its way out. Although they conducted a thorough investigation, the Jaycees never did find the cause of the noise.

They also couldn't explain how on one particular night their stereo kept turning itself off. On that evening, the coordinator and a friend were listening to sounds they had brought in to scare the children when the stereo went dead. They were confused because they were the only ones in the mansion at the time. Upon closer inspection, they found that the stereo had been turned off. They turned it back on, but the machine was again deactivated by unseen forces. Perhaps the spirit felt that if anyone was going to haunt the Hannah House, it would be him.

When a film crew came to the home in October 1981, a cameraman playfully commented how weird it would be if the dining room's chandelier began to swing. No sooner had the words come out of the man's mouth than the light fixture began to sway back and forth.

Flabbergasted, the crew watched the chandelier moving on its own. Obviously, some spirit had taken the cameraman's ill-considered comment seriously. That spirit had a sense of humor, at least.

Haunted House in Gaston

Just outside of Gaston is an old, weathered farmhouse that has stood for more than a century. It's been unoccupied for years, yet something disturbing is said to live within.

Recently, a man asked the owner if he could move into the aged home and, in exchange for free rent, repair its sagging floors, creaky ceilings and faulty plumbing. The owner agreed. Skilled at electrical work and carpentry, the residence's newest tenant began his labors. As the weeks passed, the house slowly but steadily began to regain a little bit of its former splendor.

But as the work progressed, the man began to feel that he was not alone. Just against the staircase wall in the room he had made his bedroom, he could feel a constant chill, one that persisted no matter how warm the rest of the room became. And he couldn't shake the feeling that he was being watched.

Perhaps to alleviate his concerns and his isolation, the man asked a friend and his wife to come and help. The men took care of the heavier work while the woman concentrated on choosing wallpaper and paint for the rooms. She considered herself something of an expert in the field, having remodeled several homes in the past. But for some reason, she was now plagued with indecision. None of the color schemes or patterns she looked at felt right.

Then, late one evening while the men were installing brace beams, the wife glanced down at the book of wallpaper samples she'd brought and was startled to see that a particular pattern, a subtle floral print with a light cream background, looked as if it had been singled out. She knew she had found her wallpaper.

That weekend, the woman began the arduous task of putting up the wallpaper. Starting in the kitchen, she was surprised at how easily the work progressed. It was almost as if "an extra set of hands was helping me," she says. She was amazed at the absence of air pockets and crooked strips. And sometimes, just out of the corner of her eye, she would glimpse a shadow moving about the room. If she looked at it directly, it would disappear. To the young wife, the shadow was there to assist. In two days she was finished, and the farmhouse began to look like a home.

As time progressed, the tenant became more and more disgruntled with what he perceived to be unwelcome spirits inhabiting his house. He claimed that cabinet doors would slam shut on his hands by themselves, outside doors would mysteriously lock on their own and his pets avoided every room but the kitchen. He confided to his friends that he believed an old woman haunted the house and that she was upset with him and would stand in front of the wood stove and glare at him.

It was obvious to his friends why the spirit, if it did indeed exist, would be aggravated with the tenant. The wood stove was the house's only source of heat, and to feed it the tenant had begun pulling down the interior walls of the farm's barn. Whoever was standing in front of the man's wood stove obviously had a deep connection to the barn and was far from happy to see it destroyed in such a manner.

The tenant decided that he'd had enough of both the house and Indiana. He started making plans to relocate to the sunnier climes of Florida. When his friends learned of

A ghostly grandmother haunted an Indiana farmhouse.

the impending move, they decided they wanted to buy the house. They'd spent so much time renovating and refinishing the place that it already felt like home. They made the owner an offer and he accepted. Within weeks, the couple and their children moved in.

The wife found the setting up of her new home to be very odd. Over the years she'd become accustomed to furnishing her bedroom in a specific way, but this time, it was as if she was being directed as to where all her furniture should go.

Within days, everything was unpacked. The couple called the owner and asked if he would come by to sign the purchase papers. The owner agreed. He mentioned that he was curious to see the place, as he had not set foot in it since his grandmother had died there.

When the owner arrived, he was shocked speechless. The wife, seeing his reaction, asked him if everything was all right. The owner finally stammered out a question: "How did you possibly restore that wallpaper? I can't believe it!" The wallpaper pattern of a subtle floral design on a light cream background was the same as the one that had decorated the walls of the home when the owner's grandmother had lived there.

As the owner walked through the restored home, he could not believe other startling resemblances. Lace curtains on the windows were the same as his grandmother's. The furniture was arranged in the same manner as his grandmother's was. The paints the wife had chosen were the same colors as his grandmother's. The couple's bed, against the staircase wall in the bedroom, was where the grandmother had had her bed, the bed in which she had died. It was as if the owner had taken a step back in time. Eerily, it seemed apparent that a spirit had guided the home's reconstruction.

As the months passed, the spirit began to make its presence felt, and the couple began to experience marital problems. The husband broke his vow of fidelity and engaged in an extramarital affair. The wife discovered his liaison. Furious, she went off to bed and, lying there, began to speak into the empty room.

As the wife laid out her distress, the chill that haunted the bed began to dissipate and was replaced with comforting warmth. The wife felt a sense of contentment and soon drifted off to sleep, wrapped in the gentle embrace of the spirit she called Granny.

The next morning, the wife awoke to find her husband sitting in the bedroom, staring blankly across the room. Apparently, he'd had his own encounter with Granny, but his was decidedly different.

As the man had sat on the living room couch the previous evening, a shadow had appeared and taken on the shape of an old woman walking across the room towards him. The husband tried to call out to his wife but found that he could muster no voice. He attempted to move but found that he could only sit there paralyzed, watching as the apparition came closer and closer. Finally, the ghost stood in front of him, glaring. The husband sat helpless as the phantom pinched his cheeks, slapped him and pulled his ears.

While the husband found the incident petrifying, his wife found it rather amusing. Despite her husband's wishes to leave the "demon house," she insisted they stay. The couple lived in the home another year and a half. And whatever the spirit had done, it had served as a warning to the husband, for he spent the rest of their time there free of any sort of extramarital affairs.

Sadly, Granny couldn't stop the inevitable; the couple divorced and eventually moved from the home.

The farmhouse was a place of heartache and betrayal for the wife, but because of the presence of one particularly concerned spirit, she looks back at her stay there with fondness and some remorse. She'll never forget that as she walked out of the home for the last time, she heard a mournful sigh, the expression of loneliness from a doting spirit.

Dewees Mansion

The Dewees Mansion in Terre Haute was once the city's best-known haunted house. For years before the home was destroyed, townspeople claimed that a spirit rose nightly from its fireplace and stalked the mansion.

The house was built in the early 19th century by Major George Dewees, a native of France, who settled with his wife and child in the community of homesteads that had sprung up along the Wabash River. Dewees was rumored to be a slave trader. He was said to be extremely gruff, a man who cherished his privacy and guarded his home with vicious dogs.

Life for the Dewees family wasn't especially idyllic. Indian activity was still strong in Indiana and during one particular skirmish, Dewees's son was scalped and killed. His death was the beginning of the end of any happiness the Dewees family might have had.

Unable to fill the void left by their child's demise, the Deweeses turned on each other in anger. They fought constantly until finally, unable to escape the misery that had taken over her life, Mrs. Dewees asked for a separation. Mr. Dewees agreed to the idea—at least until the papers were drawn up.

At this point things get a little foggy. It appears that Mr. Dewees never intended to let his wife leave. He had lost his son, and he wasn't going to lose his son's mother, too. Faced with her steadfast refusal to reconcile, Mr. Dewees got desperate. And Mrs. Dewees was never seen or heard from again.

Those who asked Mr. Dewees what had happened to his wife were greeted with the same answer: she had left the state and returned to the South. But this reassurance sounded hollow to the townspeople and they became convinced that Mr. Dewees had murdered his wife.

It was later discovered that a fireplace in one room of the mansion had taken on an odd appearance. Those who had been in the house before remembered that the fireplace had been bordered on both sides by cupboards. Now, strangely, one side had been walled over in brick.

The curious became convinced that here was a tomb of sorts, the final resting place of the vanished Mrs. Dewees. One account even reported that a probing of the column released a foul, musty odor—perhaps the smell of a decomposed body. The townspeople became further convinced after individuals began reporting strange incidents in the home, such as footsteps issuing forth from seemingly empty rooms and doors opening of their own accord.

No major investigation of the mansion was ever launched, and in the late 20th century the house became the victim of arsonists. Firefighters were able to save it before it was completely destroyed, but few in Terre Haute had either the money or the inclination to rebuild the parts that had burned down.

When it came time to finish the job the arsonists had begun, workers were apparently instructed to keep their eyes open for anything unusual within the structure's crumbling walls. Nothing was reported.

It appears that the mystery of the Dewees Mansion at 13 Poplar Street has vanished like a puff of smoke.

Greene County Log Cabin

In western Greene County, at the end of a gravel lane, lies a small cemetery, the final resting place of 19th-century children who fell victim to hardships and disease. These children undoubtedly wept as they struggled for their lives, and it is said they continue to cry even now, years after their corporeal forms breathed their last.

A short distance from the cemetery is a log cabin with a long history and an eerie present. A young family moved into the home in the 1970s, and a year later, the wife gave birth to a girl. It was at about this time that the family began to hear the cries.

In the middle of the night the mother would waken, thinking that her baby was crying. She'd gently push open her daughter's bedroom door and quietly pad into the room. To her surprise she'd find the child fast asleep. Yet there was undeniably the sound of an infant weeping.

And the crying wasn't the only sound to be heard. In one room of the house, a banjo leaned up against a wall. One day the family was reclining on a sofa in another room when something began playing the instrument. They thought it was one of their four cats rubbing up against the banjo, but when they went into the room to see for themselves, the cats were nowhere to be seen.

The young family was never terrified by these unexplained occurrences, and they do not begrudge their time in the haunted cabin. But another previous tenant of the home swears she'll never live in a haunted house again.

This woman and her husband had resided in the cabin for just a few months when strange events began taking place. The two would be lying in bed when the tones of an instrument, perhaps a flute or an organ, would rise from the dark silence. Sometimes accompanying the music would be the unmistakable feeling of an otherworldly presence moving its way across the room. The husband would wake up, sit upright and turn on the light, only to see nothing. His wife remembers that "he'd have this completely flat, glassy look on his face."

Looking back now, the woman feels that the presence was warning her, alerting her to a tragedy in the future. It tried to reach her again a couple of nights later.

This time the wife was lying in her bed, near sleep, when once again she felt the presence. Her eyes fluttered open and fell upon the figure of a female in a long, gray-blue dress with a high collar and light brown hair pulled into a bun. The figure appeared to be speaking, attempting to communicate. And then she began to motion to the woman to follow.

The woman got up and trailed the spirit. She was led into the home's living room where something caught her eye. To her right, she was stunned to see the image of a tombstone, "a vision, more or less, of one that had been in the graveyard," she says. The woman raced to wake up her husband, and the two returned to the living room, only to find that the figure and the tombstone had disappeared.

A few months later, the woman's husband was killed in an automobile accident. The woman now sees all the events that occurred in the home as an omen, a harbinger of doom. She believes the spirit was warning her of her husband's death. Her memories of the time spent in the log cabin are understandably stained with extreme loss and grief. She claims that while she was never scared and is convinced that the spirits were in some way benevolent, she would never knowingly move into a haunted house again.

The Sheeks House

The sleepy little railroad town of Mitchell has acquired an extra resident. The first home to be built there is reportedly haunted by a spirit of unknown origins.

Situated at the point where the New Albany & Salem Railroad crossed the proposed line for the Ohio & Mississippi Railroad, Mitchell was built on property owned by a man named John Sheeks. In 1853, Sheeks sold half interest in the land to Cincinnati businessman George W. Cochran. Together they contracted Ormsby McKnight Mitchel to survey the town site.

Mitchel was a surveyor for the railroad as well as a professor of the University of Cincinnati. As payment for his service, the town was named after him. The second *l* came about later; apparently a government clerk in Washington, D.C., added it as he was entering the title in records.

The first residents of Mitchell were Sheeks and 25 to 30 families from North Carolina. The first train passed through the town in 1857. Shortly after, hotels and saloons began popping up along the railroad. Business thrived, and by 1907 Mitchell was officially declared a city.

Little is known about what happened to John Sheeks, but his home remains the subject of much conversation. Not only was it the first house to be built in Mitchell, it is also thought to be haunted.

In the 1950s, three brothers—Bill, Grover and Bob Landreth—were asked by the owners of the John Sheeks House to renovate the building. The men went about their work but were puzzled and surprised when one particular door in the home absolutely refused to stay shut.

After closing and fastening it, the brothers would repeatedly find that someway, somehow, it had forced itself ajar. Bill's son recalls his father marveling how one time he even nailed it shut only to return to find it open with the nail rolling on the floor.

One of the men's tasks was to remove the house's hearth. While doing so, they found a sack lying amid the dust and rubble. Bill's son was there, and when his father hoisted the sack, he asked whether he could have whatever it was that was rattling and clinking inside of it. His dad said yes. Bill's son took the bag, opened it and dumped its contents. His reaction grabbed the attention of all three Landreth men. They ran to the child and found him awash in a shower of riches. The bag contained gold coins.

After the gold was removed from the home, whatever it was that was haunting the John Sheeks House grew quiet. The door never opened by itself again. But for the town of 5000, where 19 trains pass through on any given day, the mystery refuses to go away. The past continues to linger, not just in the numerous antique shops in the downtown district, but also in the minds of the curious.

Flames of Mystery

As soon as the sun broke, William Hackler made his way home, sledgehammer in hand. Determined that he and his family would never spend another night in their house, he began battering away at the building's walls.

It may seem odd that this homeowner deliberately destroyed his house, but to the people of Odon, he had no other choice. The day before, as told by writer K.T. MacRorie, the Hackler family had reportedly endured the most peculiar of experiences.

The day began as any other. Mrs. Hackler prepared a breakfast of bacon and eggs while Mr. Hackler roused their children from slumber. The meal passed without incident. Then, while Mrs. Hackler was clearing away the dishes, she smelled smoke. She checked the wood stove but nothing was burning there. She worked her way through the house and realized that the smoke was coming from upstairs, pouring out from beneath a second-floor window.

Mrs. Hackler could not see flames, so she called her family to come investigate. When Mr. Hackler saw the bubbling paint, he determined that the fire was burning from within the walls. The Odon Fire Department was called, and within minutes the blaze was doused.

The firefighters were extremely puzzled. They could not find a cause for the fire. After all, the home did not have electricity, and there was no identifiable source of combustion. The blaze had seemingly started from nothing. There was little more the fire department could do. They reassured the Hacklers that the flames were out and the home was safe. They left, only to be abruptly called back to the residence within minutes of their departure.

This time a mattress in one of the bedrooms had burst into flames, burning from the inside out. Again the firefighters doused the blaze. Again they found no explanation for the flames, deemed the house safe and went on their way. And again they were called back.

The fire department had never encountered anything like this before. But it was only the beginning. By day's end, the Hacklers, the firefighters and the people of Odon would be witnesses to the impossible. In the span of three hours, nine separate fires were reported in the Hackler house.

A calendar in the kitchen spontaneously combusted, as did a pair of Mr. Hackler's overalls. The two objects were reduced to ash within seconds. A firefighter standing next to a coffee table noticed a book begin to smoke without warning. He opened the book and saw flames working their way across the pages.

By nightfall, the number of reported fires had swelled from 9 to 28. Spontaneous combustion does occur often—in piles of leaves, green hay or coal—but in overalls and books? Apparently some mischievous spirit was at work in the Hackler house that day.

That evening, Mr. Hackler resolved that his family would never set foot in the cursed place again. He and his wife and children spent the night under the stars and, when morning came, tore the house down. Using the salvaged lumber, Mr. Hackler rebuilt the home a few miles away.

It never was determined who or what had set the fires that eerie day in 1940, but since the Hacklers lived peacefully in their new house, it is believed that the spirit was not haunting the building but the land. The spirit evidently decided not to follow the family it had tormented.

Those who doubt these incidents ever took place need only to look at the April 19, 1941, issue of *Colliers,* in which the Traveler's Insurance Company made the Hacklers' experience the centerpiece of an ad, not surprisingly, for home fire insurance.

Haunted in Bicknell

A decade ago, a newly married couple, eager to embark on their pursuit of the American dream, purchased their very first home. And in doing so, they acquired a very interesting roommate.

According to information provided by Vincennes University, the pair settled down in Bicknell, a little community nestled between Terre Haute and Evansville. The house they bought was older and partly furnished. The previous owners had died, and surviving family members had sifted through their furniture, taking some items, leaving others behind.

The couple moved in and quickly decided that since there were two bedrooms and they needed only one, the spare room would be converted into a dining room. A magnificent square oak dining table was taken from the kitchen and put into the new room. Other pieces were moved, too, and that was when the newlyweds began to notice something rather odd.

Every time an item was relocated—be it a table or a chair or an antique—the pair would hear footsteps. It was as if an invisible being was walking around the displaced object. Rather than being frightened by this eerie sound, however, the couple simply concluded that their house was haunted and that the spirit was none other than the previous owner, a man curious to see how his former home was faring in the hands of new tenants.

After the moving and renovations were complete, the couple settled into their new life. Often, the house was left empty as both worked during the day and, at times, were called away on business for weeks on end. But when the two were at home, they could always count on a surprise visit from their spirited friend. He became an integral part of their lives; they began looking at the ghost as part of their family.

Whenever something went missing only to turn up somewhere else, the pair simply attributed it to their ghost at work. Like the time the wife came home from work and placed her keys on top of the television, then later realized they had mysteriously vanished. Days went by before the keys suddenly and inexplicably turned up in the glove compartment of her car. The wife only shook her head and smiled.

As the years passed, the home began to feel a little small. But rather than move, the couple decided to expand. With a child on the way, another bedroom would have to be built. And while they were at it, another bathroom, a hobby room and a laundry room wouldn't hurt. Professionals were called in to do the work.

As the builders tore down walls and ripped up floors, they could hear, much like the newlyweds when they first moved into the home, phantom footsteps moving about. The spirit must have been pleased with what was happening, though, for nary a prank was played and the renovations were carried out with few problems.

Surprisingly, after everything was finished, the ghost's visits became more and more infrequent. Even when the couple gave birth to a bouncing baby boy, the spirit did not drop in as they thought he would. Instead, the ghost seemed to fade into the woodwork.

The couple now believes their spirit is content, happy to see that its home is in good hands and is once again the setting for familial joy and love. And that could be the case. But perhaps the ghost just decided that it was time to move on; that there was nothing left of his old home; that time had passed him by.

Regardless, the little family in that old home in Bicknell will forever remember the time when they were four and not just three, and will forever hope that their spirit returns for a visit.

Haunted Housemates

There is a house in Bloomington that has a shrunken head hanging over its front entrance. The grisly ornament is an ominous reminder of the eerie events that reportedly took place inside.

The house has served lots of functions over the years, but most recently it's been used as a residence for students of Indiana University. Four students moved into the home and, despite their landlord's advice not to disturb anything in the basement because illegal activities had taken place there, they decided to clean up the place. They told Cheryl Scutt of the *Bloomington Herald-Times* about their experiences.

As the students worked, they discovered a disturbing item. Hidden underneath stacks of old clothing, board games and other refuse was a cement bench. The bench was formed in the shape of a *U,* and in its center stood what could be taken as a cross. The housemates also discovered a bunch of old letters, passionate and lengthy correspondence between a man named Carl Smith and a girl who had once lived in the home. From these forgotten papers they learned that Smith had served in Vietnam and that he had perished during the conflict.

As soon as the makeshift altar and letters were found, strange things began happening in the house. One evening, as the students were cleaning out another room, they heard a most puzzling sound. They stopped what they were doing and strained to listen. The noise was coming from the television, which was extremely odd because none of them had been in the room to turn it on. It had turned itself on.

The misadventures continued when the tenants decided to use the Ouija board they had found in the home. As if tempting fate, they shut themselves in their living room and asked the board two questions. The first thing they wanted to know was how many spirits were with them. The board pointed to six. The second was where the spirits passed their time. The housemates' hands trembled as the pointer made its way across the board, slowly but surely spelling out not the name but the nickname of one of the students. The foursome turned to look at the room of that particular roommate. As if on cue, the light from underneath its closed door flickered for a brief moment and then winked out.

The Ouija board's time had come and gone, and no more questions were asked of it that night. Instead, the friends took a walk, eager to get out of the house and try to forget what they had just seen. It was an impossible task, though, for when they returned to the house, they noticed that the light in the bedroom, which had been undisturbed since they'd left, had mysteriously turned itself on again.

The television was not the only sound that disturbed the relative peace of the home. Once, while they were listening to music on their stereo, the students heard a scream tear through the air that was definitely not a part of the song. One roommate was so chilled by the experience that he refused to sleep in the house that night, retreating instead to a friend's place. At times, moans and wails were also heard from the supposedly empty basement. All of these eerie experiences have contributed to the aura of mystery surrounding the house in Bloomington.

2
Ghosts in Public

Public places are shared spaces, so it's not surprising that a number of them count among their visitors spirits who remain tethered to the corporeal plane. These locales are the backdrops against which entire lives have been acted out, so it's only natural that people developed a singular passion for them that survives even in the grave. We are creatures of habit, after all, and just as we will visit a restaurant time and time again because we enjoy its food and atmosphere, ghosts seek out the familiar and the comfortable for the same reason. We often have to remind ourselves that in the end, ghosts are not much different from us. They are the souls and spirits of the once living, subject to the same compulsions and desires as those who still draw breath. Their appearances in public places speak to their humanity.

The Gray Lady of Evansville

Patrons venturing to the Willard Library to check out a mystery could be pleasantly surprised. They might just encounter one long before they reach the front counter.

At the corner of First Avenue and Lloyd Expressway in Evansville, the Willard Library is the oldest building in Indiana. It was built in 1885 by Willard Carpenter. Carpenter was an intelligent man, although he had little formal education. He was 1 of 12 children, and left home when he was 18 to dabble in real estate speculation. He became one of the most influential Democrats in Evansville, serving as a city councilor for 30 years.

The library was the realization of Carpenter's vision. Listed on the National Register of Historic Places, the Victorian Gothic structure is a landmark, valued for its architecture, its extensive collection of genealogical records, and its wealth of papers dating back to the mid-19th century. And nestled somewhere within the stacks is said to be the spiritual remains of a woman known simply as "The Gray Lady."

The Gray Lady had a name once, but accounts differ as to who she might have been. Some believe the spirit wandered in from a nearby cemetery. Others say it is the ghost of a woman looking for her child in the library's children's room. Still others claim it is the apparition of a female who died in the building; apparently, the matron was so taken with the beauty of where she expired that she decided to stay. And finally, there are those who maintain that the Gray Lady is the ghost of Louise Carpenter, Willard's own daughter.

Rumors at the time indicated that Louise was furious when her father donated the money needed for the library's construction. Not sharing his giving nature, she sued the library's Board of Trustees in an attempt to prove that her father's generosity had been an example of his withering mind. Louise lost her suit, and it is said that upon her death, she returned to the site that caused her so much misery, refusing to leave until the property and its holdings were restored to the family.

Regardless of who the Gray Lady once was, her spirit seems to be alive and well. Its first recorded appearance occurred in 1937. It was a cold, snowy night and the Willard Library's janitor was heading to the basement to shovel coal into the furnace. Suddenly, he bumped into something.

Lost in the shadows, the janitor couldn't quite make out what he'd hit. So he turned on his flashlight and played its beam across the room, only to freeze in shock at the vision of a veiled lady dressed in glowing gray standing before him. Soon after, he left his job for less disturbing work. Another man was hired as a replacement, but within weeks he too had quit.

Since then, countless incidents within the library have been attributed to the mysterious Gray Lady. Take, for example, the strong smell of perfume that seems to emanate from nothingness. It has been described as an elegant, old-fashioned scent, musk-based and smoky. Eerily, the scent will often be perceptible in one part of a room but not at all in another.

In the late 1970s, a librarian was in the staff bathroom. At that time, there was only one bathroom for both men and women. She made sure the room was empty, locked

The Gray Lady haunts the Willard Library in Evansville, Indiana.

the door and went into the stall. Then she heard the sound of running water. She called out but silence was her only response.

When the librarian came out of the stall, she saw that both faucets were on and realized that someone or something had turned them on. After making sure the bathroom door was still locked and the room was still empty, she concluded that she had been visited by the Gray Lady.

Other unexplained events include an empty elevator going up and down and motion sensors being tripped off when the library is empty. Books fall off shelves and chairs pull themselves out. There are those who even claim that the ghost visited their homes. Jackie Sheckler of the *Bloomington Herald-Times* writes how long-time librarian Margaret Maier was convinced the Gray Lady went home with her when the library underwent construction in the mid-1980s.

In 1984, the children's wing of the Willard Library was temporarily closed. While her favorite haunt was being renovated, the Gray Lady needed alternative lodging. She apparently chose Margaret Maier as a roommate. Sheckler writes, "On her way home, Maier complained of her automobile being inexplicably cold. She also woke up cold the next morning at home" and her nostrils were treated to the strong scent of that elegant, smoky perfume emanating, seemingly, from nothingness.

For days after, unexplained phenomena began to exhibit themselves in Maier's house. Lights would turn on and off, appliances would rattle and strange sounds were heard. Maier even once saw a woman, a veiled lady in glowing gray, appear out of nowhere in her front room. She was convinced that the ghost was the Gray Lady.

After three months, the children's wing reopened and life in both the Maier household and the Willard Library returned to normal. The Gray Lady had returned, and just in time, too. In 1985, the governor of Indiana, Robert Orr, hosted a dinner for the Friends of the Library to celebrate the centennial of the Willard and "its resident spirit, the Lady in Gray." But researcher Mark Marimen notes that while many guests showed up, the guest of honor did not.

In 1985 a psychic was also brought in to determine who the Gray Lady was. The psychic said she encountered the spirit in its favorite haunt, the children's reading room, but found the ghost uncommunicative. What she could discern was that the Gray Lady probably lived sometime during the early 19th century and that the ghost was haunting not the building but the land.

The psychic saw the Gray Lady standing in an open meadow, watching her reflection in a pool of water, and thought that perhaps she had drowned. The land on which the Willard Library now stands was once an open meadow, and a canal wended its way through that stretch of land, so there is reason to believe that the psychic's instincts were correct. Unfortunately, there is no way to know for certain.

Either way, the Gray Lady continues to make her presence felt at the Willard Library. And she is as much a part of the place as its collection of 100,000 books.

Porticos Restaurant

For most people, fine dining is a good experience, a chance to sit with friends and family and forget, just for a moment, the pressures of daily life. But for patrons of the old Porticos Restaurant in Bloomington, eating in one of the most beautiful buildings in the city was unsettling to both the mind and the stomach.

Whether the odd events that happened in the restaurant were the result of too many glasses of wine or the cooks replacing the parsley with another type of green will never be known. But many believed that the towering 12,000-square-foot structure at 520 North Walnut was haunted.

According to accounts from the *Bloomington Herald-Times*, the history of the Porticos began in 1890 when Philip Kearny Buskirk, president of the First National Bank, began building his home. The Porticos Restaurant, which closed in 1992 after 12 years of business, was located in this mansion. Buskirk spared no expense in making his home the perfect showplace for his wealth.

Supporting walls of limestone were 18-inches thick, and multiple fireplaces heated the immense building. Leaded glass, oak woodwork and intricately decorated masonry were abundant, floral swags sat above the windows, and slate shingles awed all those who passed by.

But just seven years after the house's completion, Buskirk died at the age of 44. He was at home, eating lunch at his dining room table, when his body stiffened and then slumped forward.

After Buskirk's death, the mansion was sold to William Graham and then to William Showers, owner of the Showers Furniture Factory. Showers didn't like the imposing interior of the house, so he had it renovated. By 1915, local newspapers were calling the dwelling "the most beautiful in Bloomington."

In the late 1940s, the building became home to the Phi Kappa Tau fraternity, and later to Toad Hall, a furniture store. After that it housed a restaurant known as The Whimples. Then, in 1980, Dr. and Mrs. Steven Lewallen bought the place and opened up Porticos, which would go on to find acclaim as one of the finest eateries in southern Indiana.

It is with the opening of The Whimples that the reports of the unexplained began. One evening in the late 1970s, the restaurant manager left the building after spending a long and tiring day meticulously arranging place settings for a large banquet the next afternoon. He returned in the morning to his opening duties and was aghast to find that all his hard work had come undone. He could only stare in horror, mouth agape, eyes bulging. All the wineglasses he had placed on the tables the day before had been reduced to piles of glass shards. More disturbing, nothing else had been touched.

When Steve and Anita Lewallen opened Porticos, they installed a sound-activated alarm system. One night, the Lewallens were awakened by a call from the local security company. Unusual noises in the restaurant had tripped the alarm. At 3 AM audio monitors had recorded the high-pitched pleas of children imploring their parents to play with them. Sounds of a bouncing ball were also heard.

Local police sped to the restaurant. They entered, walked inside and turned on the lights. After an exhaustive search of every room, they found nothing. No children, no sign of the ball they'd reportedly been bouncing, no sign of the parents they'd asked to play. The house, save for the presence of the authorities, was empty.

Nights later, the alarm was tripped again. This time, the security company reported a radio blaring in the restaurant. They alerted the manager, who went to Porticos at 4:30 AM to investigate. Of the two radios inside, one was unplugged and the other was turned off.

One time when the restaurant was open, a woman walking up the stairs to the restroom had to turn back. Her way was blocked by two children who had locked their arms and refused to let her go by. After hearing the woman's story, Anita Lewallen hurried over to the staircase. She saw nothing. She polled her customers and discovered that there had been no children in the building that night.

On other occasions, customers would return from the upstairs bathrooms and ask Anita, "Are those your kids playing upstairs? We saw them bouncing a ball in the hallway." But when Anita would try to find the children, she'd only encounter an empty corridor.

In 1988, a radio announcer decided that he'd spend a night in the haunted building. He brought a tape recorder with him, and after making sure he was alone and all the doors and windows were locked, turned it on and settled in for some sleep. The next morning the announcer was shocked to hear (in addition to the sounds of his snoring) the voice of a young girl on the tape. He could offer no explanation as to what the voice was. He maintained that there'd been no children in the restaurant, that he'd been the only one in the building.

The "disappearing children" were only one part of the haunting of Porticos. Women using the ladies' room sometimes found themselves trapped. The door wouldn't open, even though it contained no latch or lock of any kind.

During a remodeling, workmen heard what sounded like water running in the wall between the men's room and the banquet room. A plumber was called in to open the partition. By the time he had finished, the sound of the water had stopped. Everything within was completely dry. Looking over the pipes and fixtures, the plumber determined that all the water lines had been capped off many years before.

Late one evening, Porticos manager Steve Koontz and three waiters finished up the night's accounting in a basement office, then headed up the stairs to clear the dining room tables. They found they had more than just dirty plates and glasses to clear. Three tables had been turned upside down, chairs had been scattered and dishes had been shattered all over the floor. The four staff members stood amidst the carnage, flabbergasted. They were the only ones in the building, the doors were locked, the windows sealed tight and they hadn't heard a sound.

On another night, a passerby called the Bloomington Fire Department to report smoke billowing out of the restaurant's second story. The brigade rushed to the building, fought their way past clouds of ash and soot and discovered nothing. There may have been smoke, but there was no fire.

Weeks later, a diner was fixing her hair in a hall mirror when she glimpsed smoke rising from a couch behind her. She whirled around, but the smoke had disappeared. Earlier, a waiter and waitress had been sitting on that same couch, resting their tired feet after a long evening of running food and serving drinks. The waiter suddenly jumped up and screamed. He claimed his back was on fire. The waitress leapt as well, and reaching around, felt her own back. She couldn't believe the sensation, the feeling of tremendous heat and energy. Her posterior was burning hot.

No one can say for certain what caused the strange incidents in Porticos Restaurant, but there are rumors that Buskirk's house was not the first structure built on that particular piece of land. Some claim that long ago, in the mid- to late 19th century, another home occupied the lot at 520 North Walnut. In it a young couple lived with their two young children.

Apparently, the couple often sat on the veranda and watched their kids play ball. It is uncertain what happened to them, but it is speculated that a catastrophic fire destroyed the home and the entire family. Maybe their spirits were trapped, waiting until the day another home would provide the perfect place to play. If so, they have been unusually quiet for years now. The Pinnacle Properties Management Group has owned the Buskirk Mansion since 1995, and that company has yet to experience any unusual activities. Maybe there was something in the food of Porticos after all.

Matthew Mourned

People usually visit museums to take a trip back in time, at least figuratively. But at the Jennings County Historical Society Museum, it's possible to make the journey...literally.

Years ago, perhaps sometime in the late 19th century, the museum did not exist. Instead, there was a field of green, a verdant carpet amid the brown of the wheelworn tracks of stagecoaches and the plowed farmer's fields. It was an idyllic spot, where the sounds of children at play and people at work met with those of the plains to create a simple but comforting symphony. But as is often the case, fate conspired to intrude.

At eight years of age, Matthew Philips stood 3¹/₂ feet tall and had sandy-colored hair. Physically, there was little to distinguish him from the other tousled-haired children with whom he played. Besides tag and hide and seek, Matthew and his friends loved the thrill and competition of dodge ball. They'd always come to this spot, a large open grassy area just perfect for their game.

Most mornings, Matthew would rouse himself from sleep and, trailing his blanket behind him, hoist himself up to the kitchen table. His feet would dangle from his chair, and he'd shiver a little, trying to keep warm as the last lingering threads of the evening chill hung in the air. He'd wrap his blanket around his legs and smile when his father's work-worn hand ran its way through his hair. Ripples of warmth would reach the tips of his toes and fingers when his mother leaned down, set his bowl of oatmeal in front of him, and kissed him ever so gently on the cheek.

Matthew would eat quickly, eager to get out into the sun and find out what was in store for him that day. He'd find his two friends already waiting, standing out in the dirt with their ball. Turning to his mother, he'd crane his neck and raise himself just a little more by standing on his tiptoes so he could kiss her goodbye. Then he'd run off, slapping his friends' backs as a way of greeting. Just before they'd head down the lane, he'd turn around and wave to his father and mother.

One day, Matthew was running across the field, feinting right then going left, trying to dodge the ball. His friend was ready to throw when suddenly Matthew just disappeared, as if swallowed up by the earth. Soon enough, his friends realized what had happened. Matthew had fallen into a deep hole hidden by the long grass.

It wasn't a particularly wide hole, but the danger was that the hole was fed by a spring. Matthew stood the very real chance of drowning to death. He struggled vainly, thrashing about, but in doing so, he only drove himself deeper and deeper. Before long, the tips of his sandy-colored hair were under water and the struggling stopped.

Neighbors came from far and wide to help retrieve the body. They dug as quickly as they could, but it still took two days. Matthew was placed in a tiny coffin and laid to rest. To ensure that the gruesome tragedy would never happen again, the townspeople covered the hole. In 1838, a stage coach stop was built over the place and the hole became a well. Years later, the stop fell into disuse, the museum took over the site and the stories began.

Apparently, Matthew Philips had returned from beyond the grave. As explained in *Hoosier Folk Legends*, volunteers reported hearing his little feet tread through the museum when it was empty. Others claimed that the beds in some of the exhibits always looked as if they had been slept in. It was said that the boy rested for a while after walking the halls.

Matthew's spirit has scared many people, but it does not seem as if he means any harm. Perhaps he is confused, lost, unsure of what to make of all the changes that have taken place around him. Perhaps in the Jennings County Historical Society Museum he can find a bridge to his time, to an era when life was simple, his family loved him and a game of dodge ball meant the world.

The Andrew Mansion

One of the most famous homes in LaPorte was built sometime after 1845, the year Dr. George L. Andrew came to Indiana. The mansion no longer exists, but the stories surrounding it still do.

Andrew and his wife, Catherine Piatt, daughter of one of the founders of LaPorte, built their three-story colonial on what is now the corner of I and 10th Streets. It was one of the grandest structures in the Midwest. Four towering columns rose from a veranda that stretched the width of the house, a second-floor porch overlooked a circular driveway and a sunroom was set up at the rear. Within, there were several dozen chambers, as well as five set aside above the kitchen for the servants.

There is little to suggest that during their time in the home the Andrew family experienced anything out of the ordinary. Dr. Andrew continued to work as a physician and served with distinction in the Army of the Potomac and the Army of the West during the Civil War. A garden designed by New York's Central Park landscaper Fredrick Law Olmsted was added to the mansion, containing an example of each plant native to Indiana.

When Andrew retired from practice in 1885, he and Catherine sold their house to the Dunn family. The Dunns remodeled and tore out the servants' quarters. They lived in the dwelling until 1904, when they sold it to the Gwynne family. The Gwynnes occupied the mansion from 1904 until 1948, and it was during these years that reports of hauntings started trickling in.

In interviews provided by the LaPorte County Historical Society Museum, Madeline Gwynne Kinney, former curator and a daughter of the Gwynnes, recounts how one day while she lived in the house she was cleaning an empty closet when she heard something clattering to the ground behind her. When she turned around, she saw four coins lying there: two pennies and two nickels, dated respectively 1876, 1877, 1867 and 1869. She had no idea where they came from and upon closer inspection found no holes or cracks in the walls from which they might have dropped.

Days later, during a raging blizzard, the bell at the front door rang. Mr. Gwynne, thinking it might be someone seeking assistance, rushed to the door and opened it. When he looked out, all he saw was snow. The porch was empty and there was no sign of tracks.

Kinney says she'd often hear footsteps pounding up and down the staircase, only to find no one there when she investigated. And countless mornings the family would wake up to find every door and window in the home wide open even though they'd been securely locked the night before. But rather than being frightened, Kinney says she was curious and actually enjoyed the hauntings. As she puts it, "One never knew what [the ghost] would do next."

The Zimmerman family was the last family to live in the Andrew Mansion. They, too, experienced the hauntings, but they were not as eager as the Gwynnes to embrace them. In fact, at one point, Mr. Zimmerman, exercising his constitutionally protected Second Amendment rights, bought a revolver in the hopes that it might scare away the spirit who opened and closed doors and breathed down people's necks.

An incident eerily similar to the one Kinney experienced happened to Mrs. Zimmerman as she was cleaning out a closet one day. She had removed the wallpaper, washed the walls, closed the door and gathered up her supplies when she heard the distinct sound of tinkling. She opened the closet door and found a small pile of silver coins lying in the center of the floor. She had no idea where they came from.

As before, the ghost exhibited to the family its particular fondness for ringing the doorbell. One of the Zimmermans' daughters was home alone when she heard the bell ringing. She opened the front door but found nothing. She shut the door and started walking back up the stairs when the bell rang again and again and again. She quickly scurried to the top of the stairs. When she finally worked up the courage to go back down, the front door was open and snow was blowing into the entrance.

Few, if any, are said to have actually seen the ghost responsible for these incidents. But Ginna, another of the Zimmerman girls, was out picking flowers in the garden one spring day when she felt a distinct chill and could not shake the feeling that she was being watched.

Ginna looked all around her but saw nothing until she glanced up at the house. At the attic window, she saw the figure of a woman standing and looking down upon her. No sooner had she realized what was happening than the woman disappeared. Ginna knew there were no visitors in the house that day, and a quick inspection of the attic revealed to her that nobody had been up there in years.

The Zimmermans eventually moved away, and this time no other family came to take their place. The mansion turned into a favorite haunt of thrill-seekers, who went there in search of ghosts. To summon the ghosts, these people built fires on the home's once-beautiful floors. Eventually the house was condemned, and in the early 1970s, the whole thing was torn down to make way for a medical center.

But when the gleaming new building was finally opened, it seemed that something from the Andrew Mansion had been left behind. Doctors and nurses reported elevators moving of their own accord, with doors opening and closing even though no one was pushing buttons. Custodians noted doors of bathrooms being locked from the inside though the bathrooms were empty, windowless and lacking a second exit.

No one is certain who the ghost of this building is, but a popular theory holds that before LaPorte became a settlement, the Potawatomi Indians regularly camped on the prairie lands the city sits on. Apparently, they were drawn to the area by a small pond, which they named Came and Went. At times, torrential rains would fill the pond to a great depth; at other times, the pond would be nearly dry.

In 1848, pressures of white settler migration forced the Potawatomi Indians to move to Kansas. On their journey, many groups passed by the Came and Went Pond. It is said a young Potawatomi girl became ill and died there, and she now continues to walk the land of her ancestors, perhaps amazed by the gadgets of the structures that have altered the landscape of the Came and Went Pond forever.

The Blue Lights of Skiles Mansion

An eerie glow of blue lights can still be seen at the site of a torn-down mansion in Indianapolis, and the curious continue to visit the place, in the hopes of catching a glimpse of the lights.

Years ago, Indianapolis municipal authorities demolished a rotting, dilapidated house in the city's Geist Reservoir area. In doing so they hoped to quell rumors circulating about the structure. Their goal was to drive away the inquisitive, those who flocked to the place to see for themselves if the home really did glow. But the city authorities did not succeed, for the faithful claim to see the lights still, even after the mansion's destruction.

The house of the blue lights was built by Skiles Test in the early 20th century. A child of affluence, Test was better known for his eccentricity than for operating the Circle Motor Inn and running a farm of 700 acres. He became the president of Indianapolis Motor Inns and for 10 years was a member of the board of the Indianapolis Transit System.

Test lived with his family in a farmhouse surrounded by vast grounds. From the road, the residence appeared isolated and ghostly, peeking eerily from between thick stands of trees lining the hills around it.

Though modest-looking, Test's house boasted only the very best in amenities and furnishings. It had its own power plant and water well, and its water pump fed not only the home, but also a swimming pool. The pool was solar heated, and for years after its construction it was

The ghostly blue lights of Skiles Test's house testify to his eccentricity.

quite an attraction for those in the area. After all, the luxury and the technology were unique.

Test seemed to have an unusual fondness for animals; he had 13 Saint Bernards and a great number of cats and rabbits. Perhaps in these pets he could find the companionship and loyalty that had three times eluded him in marriage. All deceased animals were buried in Test's pet cemetery. Before they reached their resting place, Test would purchase a small coffin, have a viewing, photograph them and send their pictures to his friends. And that wasn't the only odd thing he did.

When Test's home was torn down in the late 1970s, workers found an entrance to a two-mile long tunnel beneath his basement. Inside the tunnel they discovered barrels upon barrels of provisions Test had been stockpiling since 1924, along with hundreds of ration packs and thousands of dollars worth of survival equipment. In addition, numerous drums of oil, nails and staples were found in his barns arranged by size as if in a store.

Test's farm often housed many families and always had on hand a housekeeper, cook and farmhand, but the items found in the tunnel and the barns were enough to last two or three lifetimes. It seemed that, like some Egyptian pharaoh, Test was readying himself with the items necessary for a trip into the afterlife.

From the outside, there was nothing odd about Test's house until the blue lights became a permanent fixture. Sure, the eccentric man regularly decorated his home with lights according to the holidays. Orange and black lights for Halloween, red lights for Valentine's Day, and red, white and blue lights for the Fourth of July. And sure, he rather strangely chose blue lights for Christmas instead of the more obvious red and green. But it wasn't until one year, when Valentine's Day came and went and the Fourth of July passed by and the blue lights remained, that people began to wonder.

Neighbors who'd enjoyed Test's light shows began to question what could possibly compel the old man to keep those blue lights twinkling in the night sky. At long last, someone hazarded a guess, proposing that the blue lights had been a favorite of Test's late wife and that he kept them on as a sort of homage to her memory. Someone else added to the speculation, claiming that Test had placed his perfectly embalmed wife in a coffin of glass, keeping her with him always in their living room and surrounding her with a bank of blue lights.

Apparently Test's wife died during a party to celebrate the completion of his Olympic-size swimming pool. She was walking down the stairs of the three-story bathhouse when the railing gave way and she plummeted to her death. Some claimed Test believed the blue lights attracted the spirits of the dead and would bring back his wife. Others maintained it had already happened. These people contended that Test's wife, trapped between death and life, still performed her daily routines. Teenagers bold enough to approach the home even boasted that she would answer the door when the doorbell rang.

Skiles Test died in 1964, and days later an auction was held to sell off his estate. More than 30,000 people were attracted to the house of the blue lights. No one found a glass coffin containing a dead body.

Strangely, though, even after Test's death, and even after the house's power plant was shut down, people passing by the home still reported seeing the eerie blue glow. And they continue to do so now—even though the mansion has been torn down.

The Mansion

In 1981, when Mark Miles of Louisville bought a mansion in Vevay, he acquired not only the largest home in the city, but a ghost as well.

The 35-room house Miles purchased was built in 1874 by Benjamin Franklin Schenck, the richest son of Ulysses P. Schenck. Ulysses had made his fortune shipping grain, hay and feed up and down the Ohio River, and after studying law, Benjamin joined his mercantile business. Benjamin also owned and edited a weekly newspaper and was involved in the ink business.

By all accounts, Benjamin was universally respected, a man who treated others with compassion and accommodation. He was a loving father, a doting husband and a devoted son, and he lived his life guided by religious principles.

When construction began on The Mansion, it was an event grand enough to set those living in the Ohio River Valley abuzz with anticipation. As the walls went up and the full scope of the project began to assert itself, the townspeople couldn't help marveling at what would become (and remains) the largest house in Switzerland County.

The dwelling was built to reflect the second empire architecture style. It had four porches, eight chimneys, a four-story tower and countless windows. Its circular driveway stretched for a quarter of a mile. Its roof was built from slate, and its exterior trim was made of tin. Inside there were five bathrooms, each containing a walnut-cased, copper-lined bathtub.

In 1874, the house was completed, and people walking by craned their necks skywards to gaze at its size and eminence. Sadly, Benjamin wasn't able to fully enjoy the fruits of his labor. He died just three years later, having spent a mere two summers in his newly finished home.

Benjamin's daughters donated the mansion and the 65 acres it sat on to the Indiana Baptist Convention in 1923. Over the years it was used as a clubhouse for the Switzerland County Saddle Club and an orphanage. By the 1970s, it had fallen into a state of disrepair. Its 35 rooms, unoccupied for years, sagged with age. Parts of its brick walls crumbled. And its once-manicured lawns and gardens resembled a jungle.

By the time Miles acquired the property, stories of a ghost abounded. In fact, Miles experienced difficulties convincing restoration workmen to work on the house. The spirit said to dwell within The Mansion's walls was that of a woman, a tall Victorian lady with long brunette hair wearing a white dress with a high lace collar. The workers who were finally hired reported seeing the ghost many times. It was far from hostile but was definitely mischievous. Apparently it had a fondness for moving tools, turning off lights and playing with shutters.

Miles spent many nights in the mansion with the shutters open to let in the cool night air. When he'd awake, the shutters would be closed. If he'd get up in the night to go to the bathroom, lights he'd turn on en route would be eerily dark on his way back to his bed.

Seemingly the ghost of The Mansion was also a charmer. John Tedesco, Jr., the house's former caretaker's son, claims that the ghost would, at times, come behind him and kiss his neck, whispering, "You see every move

I make, don't you?" And on some of the nights that Miles slept in the house, he could sense a presence not just in his bedroom, but in his bed.

Miles never saw the spirit sleeping beside him, but he always felt that if he could have rolled over quickly enough, he would have been able to see it. Perhaps if the ghost had been as friendly with the workmen as it had been with Miles and Tedesco, there would never have been a shortage of workers to begin with.

Miles eventually sold the home to Jerry and Lisa Fisher, who now run The Mansion as a bed and breakfast. Guests looking to experience the restored splendor of Schenck's home may find their visit beyond their wildest expectations should a lovely young ghost decide to make her presence felt in the form of an unexpected nuzzle or kiss.

Burning Wood?
Must Be Homer

When some entrepreneurs had the enterprising idea to
renovate an old barn on the edge of Plymouth and turn
it into a restaurant, they certainly got more than they
bargained for. While they were delighting in their nostal-
gic trip, another individual, one distinctly not of this
physical world, was enjoying the atmosphere as well.

The Hayloft Restaurant was constructed out of a cow-
shed that was almost a century old and had been unoccupied since the 1970s. The years of neglect had taken
their toll on the building's walls, beams, siding and roof,
but by the time it opened again as an eatery, it was
restored to near original condition.

Patrons would come in, sit amidst the antiques and
enjoy plates of comfort food of the highest order: prime
rib and barbecue baby back ribs. But after the restaurant
had been open for some time, people who ate there
became aware that they were not dining alone.

There are a number of guesses as to who haunted the
restaurant. Most agree that it was a farmer with some
unfinished business. Some say the man was brutally murdered on his land; others claim he was consumed in a
ghastly fire. Those of a less suspicious nature believe that
the ghost is that of a man named Jacob who simply
expired at the back door of his barn when his clogged
arteries gave way.

Either way, the old farmer did not appear to mean
anyone harm; he simply moved furniture around, rattled
wine glasses and had a fondness for turning lights on and

off. He was helpful, pushing objects out of people's ways, and he was mischievous, rattling plates when taunted.

Some believe that the apparition answered when called. Staff christened the spirit Homer, and when that name was mentioned, things seemed to happen. Pots and pans fell from their racks, or glasses cracked and broke. Homer himself sometimes appeared, as a middle-aged man wearing overalls, looking for all intents and purposes like an Indiana farmer. Except for one small fact—most farmers have feet. Homer's ghost had a head, a body and arms, but when it came to legs, he was just thigh.

The footless wonder was sighted many times, often in the upstairs dining room called the Silo Room. Frightened busboys and experienced staff reported seeing the ghostly farmer appear from the room's stairwell, walk into the room and then just fade away.

But he was also seen in the kitchen, and sometimes, perhaps when seeking a bit of fresh air, in the parking lot. Just before the ghost appeared, the restaurant was overwhelmed by an earthy odor, which many described as smelling like "burnt, wet wood."

Unfortunately, fire ravaged the Hayloft Restaurant in April 2001. Damage was extensive and it's not known whether the restaurant will reopen. And that is too bad—for the people of Plymouth seem to have embraced the eatery's spirit as their own version of a homegrown celebrity.

Culbertson Mansion
State Historic Site

Those who visit the Culbertson Mansion State Historic Site will marvel at its splendor. And they'll be even more amazed at its collection of sprightly spirits.

In 1867, in New Albany, construction began on a home that would come to be considered the very definition of affluence. Designed by local architect James T. Banes, the house reflected the grandeur of the French Second Empire style. It had three stories, contained 20,000 square feet of living space, included 25 rooms and cost the builder $120,000. Its interior boasted fabric-quality wallpapers, marble fireplaces and woodwork intricately carved and detailed by local boat builders. Its tin roof was imported from Scotland.

The mansion belonged to William Stuart Culbertson of New Market, Pennsylvania. According to the New Albany Historical Society, Culbertson was 21 when he left his hometown and headed west, moving into the expanding territories along the Ohio River. He finally settled in New Albany, where he found work in a dry goods store.

By 1860, Culbertson had begun to amass his fortune, expanding into wholesaling and selling products all over the Midwest. Eight years later, he left dry goods and began investing heavily in new ventures. He owned managing stock in the Kentucky-Indiana Railroad Bridge Company and opened a local utility company.

At his death in 1892 at the age of 78, Culbertson was the president of the First National Bank and presided over a fortune of $3.5 million. Adjusted for inflation, he was the proud owner of the equivalent of $61 million in today's dollars.

The people of New Albany saw Culbertson as a great philanthropist and builder. He funded the construction of the Culbertson Old Ladies Home and was trustee for the First Presbyterian Church. After the death of his second wife, Cornelia, he founded the Cornelia Memorial Orphans Home. He was also involved in the construction of the Kentucky-Indiana Railroad Bridge, the first elevated structure to span the Ohio River between New Albany and Louisville, Kentucky.

But despite the outward signs of his success, Culbertson's personal life was tinged with tragedy and loss. He married his first wife in 1840, but she died from typhoid two years before construction on his home began. He married a schoolteacher and widow in 1867, but she succumbed to cholera 13 years later. Then he married a woman from Kentucky who was half his age, but their home life was far from idyllic.

Culbertson and his third wife were allegedly strict parents, folks who locked their young children in a closet when they misbehaved. And their stiffness did not end when the kids were grown. Apparently, they found many issues over which to butt heads.

Culbertson was said to clash repeatedly with his daughters, notably Blanche and Anne, over marriage and questions of independence. The former wanted to wed a Frenchman, but her father vehemently opposed the union. The latter sought desperately to leave the house before she was united in matrimony.

In addition to the tension that was felt in the dwelling, there were constant reminders of death. An elderly aunt had died in the master bedroom. Culbertson's second wife, Cornelia, had passed in another room. And Culbertson's son Walter had expired in the building as well. The tenuous grasp on peace within the home left a legacy that continues to haunt the site to this day.

Staffers at what is now the Culbertson Mansion State Historic Site have reported various disturbances throughout the building. These include an elderly, gray-haired woman mysteriously roaming the halls, the sound of footsteps on the magnificent rosewood staircase when the home is empty, lights turning themselves on and off, the smell of pipe smoke mysteriously emanating from the formal parlor and a man's voice coming from nothingness in the front hall. In addition, a harp in the formal parlor has been said to turn itself all the way around, which is eerie, considering that the weight of the instrument demands the strength of two strong men to move it.

But perhaps the best known of the reported hauntings is an incident that took place a number of years ago. Occasionally the site is rented out to wedding parties, and at one particular reception, helium-filled balloons were used as decorations. At 10 PM, guests began leaving the home. One visitor asked if he could take some of the balloons with him. But as he was leaving, he lost his grip on the balloons and they floated up to the 15-foot high ceiling.

Later that evening, the curator of the site was awakened by a phone call. She was told the motion detectors had been tripped. The curator drove to the house, believing that the balloons were the culprits. But when she entered the building and looked up to the ceiling, she could not see the balloons. They were up in a second-floor room. How they got there was a mystery.

The balloons had somehow floated across the ceiling to the staircase, up the stairs, down the hallway and into the room through a doorway that was five feet below ceiling level. They then floated across the room and entangled themselves on a dress that had been put on display, one that had belonged to Anne Culbertson. The balloons had followed an impossible trajectory. Perhaps some spirit liked the decorations as much as the guest with the poor grip did.

Why these spirits continue to haunt the Culbertson Mansion is a mystery. Who they were in life is a riddle, too. One thing is sure, though. Should they be willing, they could easily add another unexpected dimension to this trip through time.

Taggart and French Lick

The 2600-acre Hoosier National Forest is home to the French Lick Springs Grand Hotel. The hotel boasts 485 guestrooms, an 800-seat convention hall and a 2500-seat exhibition hall. Its grounds had two golf courses, two swimming pools and mineral baths. The resort is over a century old and its beauty is unrivaled within the state—as is its fabled history.

French traders established the first outpost in the French Lick area more than 200 years ago. They discovered that rich mineral springs dotted the land and sought to profit from the large salt deposits. But in 1803, the Louisiana Purchase was finalized and the French abandoned their post. British settlers moved in and established a permanent fort.

In 1832, the lands around the mineral springs were offered for public sale. The offer lured Dr. William Bowles to French Lick. He purchased 1500 acres and within years had opened the first French Lick Springs Hotel. The hotel attracted hundreds of visitors. Most were drawn by the prospect of treating their bodies in the healing waters of the mineral springs.

Unfortunately for Bowles, his Southern sympathies in the years leading up to the Civil War led to his arrest and court-martial. As tensions mounted in the 1850s, French Lick became a key stopping point along the Underground Railroad. In response, Bowles formed a secret Confederate society called the Knights of the Golden Circle. He was accused of treason and sentenced to death.

President Lincoln eventually commuted Bowles's death sentence to life imprisonment. Bowles spent the Civil War in a federal prison in Ohio, but returned to French Lick in 1865 to resume running the hotel.

After Bowles died in 1873, many owners came and went, but the hotel continued to prosper. Then in 1897 tragedy struck. Fire swept through the complex, destroying most of the wooden buildings. Enter Thomas Taggart, the mayor of Indianapolis and head of the French Lick Springs Hotel Company.

Under Taggart's management, the French Lick Springs rose to international prominence. It was Taggart who had the idea to run daily trains from Chicago right to the front entrance of the hotel, and it was Taggart who advocated the construction of the two golf courses. It was also Taggart who became Democratic National Chairman, thereby calling the hotel and its spas to the attention of the elite of society.

Over the next 20 years, three new wings were added to the hotel. And as the hotel grew, so did Taggart's political power. He was soon recognized as the acknowledged authority of Democrat politics, and French Lick became the party's unofficial headquarters.

According to researcher Mark Marimen, it was at Taggart's hotel in 1931 that Franklin Roosevelt garnered the support necessary to secure his presidential nomination. Other visitors of note included John Barrymore, Clark Gable, Bing Crosby and the Trumans.

Taggart died in 1929 and his son, Thomas Taggart, Jr., took over. But the hotel was not immune to the ravages of the Great Depression, and few during this period had a visit to it high on their list of priorities. In 1949,

Taggart's son sold the hotel to a New York syndicate. It is now owned by the Boykin Lodging Company, which has spent years and millions of dollars restoring it to its previous grandeur. And some say that the man who made the French Lick Springs Grand Hotel has reclaimed his place there, even after his death.

Marimen has uncovered a number of incidents that have led people to whisper that Tom Taggart still walks the grounds and hallways of the hotel. In his life, Taggart was known to enter an elevator first to hold the doors open for customers or porters behind him carrying luggage. Seventy years after his death, employees carrying armloads of suitcases struggle not to drop their loads in surprise when elevator doors mysteriously open and stay open, on their own, until all are comfortably packed into the compartment.

Sometimes, the elevator will be filled with the scent of pipe and cigar smoke although smoking is strictly prohibited. And occasionally, a spectral form lingers in the lift, only to disappear before stunned individuals.

One time, a porter was carrying luggage to the elevator when the doors opened by themselves. It had happened to him once before, so he simply shrugged it off and got into the compartment. He pressed the button for the second floor, but the elevator went straight past the second floor and on to the third. When the doors opened, he was ready to hit the button for "2" again when he happened to glance down at the luggage tags. The bags were supposed to be sent to room 320. Taggart was watching, ensuring that service did not lapse even in his death.

It is not just the elevator that seems to be haunted by the lingering spirit. The sixth floor is also said to be a hotbed of ghostly activity. Staff members are nervous about working on that floor after nightfall. Many have reported feeling a presence there and seeing a fleeting shadow appear and disappear in the recesses of the hallways. Equipment supposedly turns itself on and off. The sounds of footsteps apparently echo down the hall. A phone often inspires confusion.

Staff members at the main desk sometimes receive calls from a certain room, yet when they answer there is no response. The mysterious aspect about all this is that these phantom calls often take place when no guests are registered in that particular room.

One time, the room was closed and its phone disconnected. Sure enough, the calls continued. Eeriest of all, when the empty room is called, the phone will be picked up, and all that will be heard is the sound of the room's air conditioner whirring and whistling—and nothing else.

The hauntings continue, but for all that the spirits have done, no one at the hotel seems to feel threatened. The ghost or ghosts have simply added to the atmosphere of the historic place, and have made working and staying at the hotel a little more comfortable.

State Theater Lounge

When Ken Allen purchased the State Theater Lounge in South Bend eight years ago, he bought more than just a nightclub. He didn't realize it, but included in the deal was a ghost.

The spirit has brought much attention to the lounge, most of it unwelcome. Allen and his wife worry that the specter will deter patrons from visiting their establishment, but there doesn't appear to be much to fear. The ghost has done nothing to lead the owners, employees or patrons to conclude that it is malicious. It seems to be mischievous but harmless.

As to who the spirit actually is, there are few solid ideas. It is definitely that of a woman, for it is said to wear a dress, either lavender or white. And it is reportedly quite stunning, with long brunette hair and a beautifully clear complexion. Allen believes the woman to be a flapper from the Roaring Twenties, a vaudevillian singer or dancer who performed in shows that were immensely popular in the state during the heady times of the post-war era.

The mysterious apparition often appears when the lounge has a blues-type band playing on its stage. When it surfaces, it is usually as a blur of movement. But the first time the Allens encountered it, it was completely clear.

After they took ownership of the club, the Allens hired the Fremont Theater Supply Company to install audio and video equipment. One day, Richard Smith, the man sent to do the job, had just finished his work in the projection booth. He glanced up towards the balcony for a second and realized all too suddenly that he was staring at the vision of a beautiful woman dressed in white. Within seconds, the girl vanished, leaving the confused workman and the puzzled Allens in her wake.

Some patrons who have seen the ghost appear during shows have been frightened by the vision. It falls to the Allens to reassure these particular customers that the apparition is just another part of the State Theater Lounge—to convince them that the spirit means well and, like them, is just there to enjoy the music.

3
Haunted
Universities

Everyone knows about the three Rs, but maybe it's time to talk about the three Es. Universities are about experience. They're about education. And sometimes, they're about the ethereal. While students attend these institutions with the intention of furthering an education in a chosen field, be it English or Physics, they sometimes discover learning opportunities not available in any course. A bar, dormitory room or library might be the first place a student encounters the paranormal. Universities are fertile ground for ghost stories, and it's difficult to know which stories have been exaggerated and which have not. Regardless, the stories are there, as much a part of the institution as the student union or a fraternity or a sorority. Some students go through their entire academic careers without ever experiencing the ethereal. They'll toss off the stories as myth or legend, just fodder for a rainy night. Others know better. Those who've encountered the paranormal know that inside that library, beyond that dorm room door, and down the hall lurks something very real, something that won't be discussed in a medical text or an academic journal. They'll have seen something that will linger in their memories far longer than anything they learned in class.

Return of the Gipper

One of the most famous residents of the University of Notre Dame's Washington Hall was—and perhaps still is—sports legend George Gipp.

Gipp, quite possibly the greatest all-round player in college football history, was a varsity athlete at Notre Dame from 1917 to 1920. He lived in Washington Hall the entire time. According to Mark Marimen, author of *Haunted Indiana*, his spirit may reside in the dormitory still.

Gipp was born on February 18, 1895, in Laurium, Michigan. He was the seventh of eight children and, by all accounts, a natural athlete. He had speed and agility and a competitive fire that burned brightly.

In 1916, Gipp headed to Notre Dame with ambitions of playing baseball. But one afternoon Knute Rockne, the coach of the Fighting Irish, spotted him drop-kicking a football 60 and 70 yards just for the fun of it. The persuasive coach convinced Gipp to try out for his team instead.

Gipp experienced nothing but success on the gridiron. In fact, he proved to be the most versatile player Rockne had ever had. He could run, pass and punt. He led his team to 20 consecutive wins and 2 Western Championships. But sadly, his career was cut short.

Playing against Indiana University in 1920, Gipp began to feel ill with a sore throat and chills. He lay in bed for a week, hoping to improve, and rose again only to compete against Northwestern University. He played exceptionally well that game, but observers could see that he was ailing.

On November 23, Gipp was admitted to St. Joseph's Hospital and diagnosed with pneumonia and a serious

George Gipp, Notre Dame University's famous ghost in residence

streptococcic infection of the throat. Despite treatment, his condition worsened. Finally, on December 12, his family and Rockne were sent for. It was then that Gipp, already feeling the cold grip of death, famously implored his coach to "win one for the Gipper."

Two days later, Gipp lapsed into a coma and died. On December 17, the entire student body of Notre Dame came out to watch his casket being loaded onto a train for Calumet, Michigan. While his body rests forever in Calumet, some say his spirit remains in South Bend.

Early in 1921, Jim Clancy was practicing his trumpet in Washington Hall's music room when he heard a strange, eerie sound resembling a low moan coming from the other side of the chamber. Startled, he got up and tried to locate the source of the noise. He found it coming from a tuba resting against the wall.

Clancy approached the tuba, and immediately the moaning stopped. Thoroughly spooked, Clancy grabbed his music and began to rush out of the room. But before he could exit the chamber, he was stopped in his tracks, for the instrument began playing again.

Within days, other residents of Washington Hall also heard the unearthly sound. Joe Shanahan, sneaking back into the building one night, passed the band room as he headed for the staircase. At that exact time, a low moan broke the silence. Shanahan, his breath caught in his throat, slowly turned towards the sound. Immediately, he caught a glimpse of what he called a "gossamer haze." Terrified, he fled to his room.

As the weeks and months wore on, the moans became more and more common. And they began to be accompanied by the sound of footsteps. Students whispered about doors closing on their own and things disappearing from their rooms. And one person even reported that a ghost pushed him while he walked down the stairs.

In the mid-1970s, after some people claimed to have seen the spirit of George Gipp riding on horseback on the steps of Washington Hall, a group of curious students decided to launch a ghostly investigation. The students had heard the stories and were determined to prove the phenomenon's existence.

Armed with cameras and recording devices, the students broke into the hall. They were trying to be discreet but were unable to set up their equipment in the dark, so they had to turn on the lights. But the lights wouldn't stay lit. The light switch flicked itself off immediately after it was flicked on.

Other odd things happened, too. Flashes from cameras began to fire on their own, and the air was filled with a mournful wail. Eventually, the students were filled with terror and ran away. They'd definitely found what they were looking for.

But although that particular group of students was frightened, it didn't seem that the ghost was intent on scaring those who entered Washington Hall. In the late 1970s, a group of theater students with an interest in the paranormal decided to stay late in the building and hold a seance in an attempt to contact the spirit. They used a Ouija board and asked whether or not there was a spirit in the hall who wanted to speak with them. They received a puzzling, cryptic message: "SG—Goodbye."

Confused, the students asked the question again. They got the same result. Uneasy about the situation, the budding thespians packed up and left. They heard footsteps

Washington Hall, home of George Gipp's mischievous ghost

behind them and, once outside, they dove into the bushes. Seconds later, a Notre Dame security guard stepped from the building. According to Marimen, the students claim to this day that SG stood for security guard, and that the spirit that walked the staircases of Washington Hall had been offering up a warning.

Today Washington Hall serves as the university theater. Those who occupy its rooms and offices claim that if the building was ever haunted, it certainly isn't now. Regardless, the mere mention of the name George Gipp continues to bring to mind the young man's life, his stellar football career and, of course, the possibility that he continues to cause mischief in his old stomping grounds from far beyond the grave.

Frightful Fraternity

When 625 North Jordan in Bloomington was occupied by an Indiana University fraternity, it was a dark and dreary place. It struck fear in the hearts of the fraternity brothers.

The house was surrounded by trees and enveloped in shadows. And according to the journal *Indiana Folklore*, it showed signs of being haunted.

In early September one year, Danny Jackson returned to the building to start a new semester. It was empty. Yet as he walked up the stairs to his room, he heard footsteps on the second floor. "Who's there?" he called out. But he got no response. "Who's there?" he called again.

Jackson got to the top of the stairs and turned the corner. He was greeted by—nothing. The footsteps had stopped, and there was no one to be seen. Jackson paused for a moment, wondering what was going on, and then he felt someone or something tap him on the shoulder. He was so spooked he went into convulsions. His body shook uncontrollably until some friends found him and led him to a health center.

Additional eerie incidents occurred in the house. Larry Minnix, a one-time student at Indiana University, reported faucets turning themselves on and off and phones mysteriously dialing themselves. Others claimed to hear invisible babies crying. Another Indiana University student said he walked into the bathroom late one night and found a man he'd never laid eyes on before shaving and washing himself.

Apparently, the student just stood and stared at the man. As he watched, the stranger finished what he was doing, left the room and began walking down the stairs. The student followed. But when he reached the stairs, there was no one there. The strange man had vanished into thin air.

The fraternity brothers attributed the odd incidents in the building to the spirits of those who used to live and work there. Apparently, sometime in the first half of the 20th century, the original owner of the house shot himself dead in a small room in the basement. Adding to the already sorrowful atmosphere, a medical doctor later used the home as an office in which to help young women of Bloomington rid themselves of unwanted pregnancies.

The doctor found more than enough business, but his practice was far from sanctioned, and one day he made a terrible, tragic mistake. During a botched operation, he killed a mother and her baby. While the missing baby might not have been noticed, the missing woman certainly was. The doctor was arrested, and the building was taken over by the university. Years later, even after the doctor died, people would say that it was his ghost haunting the dark corners and stairways of the house. It was thought that it was his ghost that sent fraternity pledge Danny Jackson into convulsions of fear.

The fraternity brothers took advantage of the frightening atmosphere for the initiation rites they subjected new pledges to. Young pledges were forced to spend a night in the basement, after following the stairs down, turning left and continuing all the way back to the steel doors. In such an eerie atmosphere, pledges felt a presence, an unmistakable sense of dread. Seeing the brick walls and arrows pointing to a distorted cross on the wall, they thought about all the stories they'd heard. They wondered if, as the legends suggested, the bodies of babies had been left by the doctor behind the big steel doors. They wondered if it was possible to hear the phantom sounds of babies crying. They couldn't help themselves from leaning in ever so slowly to the walls, listening for the fabled whispers, before realizing they really didn't want to hear anything. They wondered how they could be expected to spend the night there, trapped with the rumors and whispers of past years.

At one time, the president of the fraternity conducted seances in the basement. Some university students told stories of a frightening and inexplicable phenomenon involving mysterious music. These students would be awakened in the night by sounds of a record spinning slowly on the turntable in their rooms. The students could not explain this event as the stereos were not on when they went to bed, and no one could have entered their locked rooms.

The fraternity no longer occupies 625 North Jordan as the chapter disbanded in the early 1970s. The house is now home to Indiana University's Career Development Center. The doctor has not been seen in years, and the cries of the unborn have been silenced.

Stokely Mansion

Stokely Mansion is an oddity among the buildings that dot the Marian College campus. Something or someone calls the house home, and it's definitely not a student.

The mansion was built in 1912 by Frank H. Wheeler, an automotive industrialist and one of the founders of the Indianapolis Motor Speedway. Although the house was luxurious, Wheeler was not happy there. He suffered from depression and eventually killed himself in the master bedroom.

After Wheeler's death, the home was owned by a series of families. Then, in 1963, it was sold to Marian College in Indianapolis. But before the house could host the school's music department, it had to be cleaned up. Nuns were brought in to do the job.

Immediately after their arrival, the sisters realized that something in the mansion wasn't quite right. Beautiful gardens surrounded the house, and the nuns were so taken with the flowers that they festooned the home with them. But every morning when they returned to work, they would find their wonderful arrangements strewn about the floor like confetti. Eventually—unwilling to continue upsetting whatever entity was roaming the halls—they stopped putting the bouquets out.

When the nuns were finished readying the mansion, the music department moved in. And the strange occurrences continued. In addition to oddities involving lights, security guards reported hearing pianos being played late into the night. The guards would walk up the stairs to the practice rooms, but on the way the music would stop.

They'd inspect the rooms but find them eerily empty. Stranger still, when the guards went back to the front door of the building, the music would start all over again.

One night, a guard noticed that a third-floor door was open. Now, an open door is not usually cause for concern, but this particular door was the type that closed on its own and had to be propped to stay open. The guard, thinking burglary or otherwise, called the Indianapolis Police Department. Officers arrived with a dog team and, as they did, the third-floor door suddenly slammed itself shut.

The police dogs heard the door slam and tore up the steps. But when they reached the third-floor landing, they stopped. Though they were bred to hunt and chase, they refused to go farther. So the police officers went up, but they found nothing. Everything was exactly as it should have been.

The same cannot be said for other rooms in the music department. Students at Marian College discovered that the temperature in specific rooms in the building changed according to the key of the music being played within them. If the music was played in a minor key, the room would get cold. If it was played in a major key, the room would become noticeably warmer. Perhaps if the music department had exploited this phenomenon fully, the college would have saved on utility bills.

In addition to rising and falling temperatures, some faculty and students reported the appearance of Wheeler himself in the building. Apparently he looked resplendent in a double-breasted suit, smoking a cigarette. Then he vanished into thin air. Whether or not he was responsible for the occurrences in the building, however, was unknown.

As for the mansion, the music department no longer has its offices there. It's still a building for the Marian College campus, but it appears that it is, has been and always will be the home of Frank H. Wheeler.

Earhart Rises Again

When famed aviatrix Amelia Earhart disappeared over the Bermuda Triangle on July 2, 1937, searchers probed 1000 square miles of sea in search of her with no success. But maybe the searchers had their sights set in the wrong place. Maybe they should have cast their glances inland, way inland, to the Midwest.

Today, Earhart's spirit is said to reside at Purdue University in Lafayette. Apparently in death she has returned to the place where she was happiest in life.

Earhart's connection with Purdue began in the fall of 1935 when she was invited to New York City by the *New York Herald Tribune* to speak at a conference dealing with "Women Changing the World." At the time, Earhart was already a celebrity. Three years earlier she had become the first woman to fly across the Atlantic Ocean alone.

In recognition of her lofty accomplishment, Earhart had received two prestigious awards: France's Cross of the Legion of Honor and the National Geographic Society's Gold Medal. So when she stepped up to the podium to present her speech, she found herself before a rapt audience.

Earhart spoke for an hour, and one particular member of the audience listened intently. Dr. Edward C. Elliott was the president of Purdue University and was deeply interested in aviation. Elliott also worked tirelessly to grant women greater access to higher education and was troubled that just 1000 of his 6000 students, and few of his instructors, were women.

The ghost of pioneer pilot Amelia Earhart haunts Purdue University.

Earhart was the symbol Elliott was looking for. She was an individual who could champion both of the president's causes. In November of that year, Elliott invited Earhart to become a visiting faculty member of Purdue's Women's Careers Department and an advisor to the Aeronautics Department. She accepted and, according to her husband, George Putnam, "she found her time at Purdue as one of the most satisfying adventures of her life."

While she was at Purdue, Earhart announced and prepared for her infamous attempt to fly around the world. This announcement was significant for two reasons: Earhart was the first woman to take on this challenge, and her route, unlike those of others who had already circled the globe, followed the equator, the longest path possible.

Earhart started her journey in June 1937. She flew eastward from Miami, Florida, accompanied by Frederick J. Norman, a navigator. Unfortunately, her plane disappeared on July 2, while en route from Lae, New Guinea, to Howland Island. An extensive search by the United States Navy failed to discover any trace of the lost flyers.

Years later, rumors began circulating around the Purdue campus that Earhart's spirit was haunting the hangar where the pilot had spent so much of her time. A student was working in the office of hangar number one when the deafening roar of an aircraft shook the ground. The student left the office and, as suddenly as it started, the roaring stopped. A check of records showed that no aircraft was fired up in that particular hangar on that particular afternoon.

Other workers in the hangar reported seeing the specter of a woman wearing gear resembling that worn

Amelia Earhart and Edward C. Elliot in front of her plane Electra

by pilots in the late 1930s. There were also rumors circulating involving the residence hall where Earhart lived while at Purdue.

According to ghost researcher Mark Marimen, some of the girls in Earhart's former dormitory claimed they could feel cold drafts blowing through the pilot's old room. Others claimed they saw the figure of a woman with short hair hanging out in the hallway. Still others said they heard the sound of a typewriter coming from an empty room late into the night. Reportedly, that time of night was Earhart's favorite time to write.

While Purdue officials remain skeptical as to the existence of Earhart's spirit, there is no question as to the power of Amelia Earhart's legacy, both in the American imagination and in the hearts and souls of the students and faculty who walk the university's halls.

Shadowwood

The 13-room brick mansion that serves as the international headquarters of the Sigma Pi Fraternity is said to be haunted. Colonel Eugene Wharf built the Georgian-style house—dubbed Shadowwood—in 1916, and apparently he's lived there ever since.

Wharf was a brave soldier who fought in both the Spanish American War and the Civil War. He loved his country and his home and made a habit of raising the American flag every morning outside his front door.

In the 1950s, Wharf gave Shadowwood and the 13 acres surrounding it to Vincennes University. In 1962, the university gave the house to Sigma Pi. It wasn't long after that that members of the fraternity began to realize the mansion was haunted by its original owner.

According to ghost story writer Arthur Myers and ghost researcher Wanda Willis, strange things routinely happened in the home. Lights turned on by themselves, desks were dragged across rooms by unseen forces, and faucets went on and off without human intervention.

In the 1980s, the house mascot, a cat named Blackie, often stared and hissed at nothingness. Those who witnessed the cat's animosity towards seemingly empty space noted that when the cat was hissing, the room's temperature dropped drastically even though all the windows were shut.

Workers in the building noted one unfortunate side effect of the ghost's presence. Whenever the spirit appeared, it left a "psychic chill" in the air, a blast of air so cold it turned steaming hot cups of coffee into freezing liquid within seconds. But for the most part, the ghost was a friendly spirit.

One woman who worked in the mansion in the 1980s said she saw the front door of the house open on its own. She also claimed she heard footsteps and, at times, her name being called out by an unmistakably male voice. In addition, photocopiers turned on and off by themselves, and papers on desks were never where workers left them.

While the hauntings were prevalent in the 1980s, in the 1990s they were few and far between. Today the executive director of the fraternity insists that the home is no longer frequented by a phantom. "The ghost has left the building," says Mark Briscoe, "he must be with Elvis somewhere."

Three or four years ago, a group of parapsychologists was brought in to determine once and for all whether there was a presence at Shadowwood. Their search revealed that the spirit that had haunted the mansion had indeed gone. Now the only mystery that remains is why the ghost of the colonel finally decided to leave his magnificent home.

A Nightmare on Third Street

In 1958, Stanley Rice, a member of the Indiana University chapter of the Kappa Delta Rho Fraternity, was killed in a tragic car accident. Although he died, he continued to be an active part of the brotherhood.

It's been said that after the collision, Rice's spirit haunted the fraternity building at 1503 East Third Street, Bloomington. Reportedly, he appeared there in a girl's eerie dream.

The incident occurred just after final exams, when most of the students had left the campus for a well-deserved Christmas break. The fraternity house manager had invited his girlfriend over for the afternoon but got called away shortly after her arrival. The manager told his girlfriend he wouldn't be gone long and left her in his room to wait for his return.

As the girl waited, she found herself getting tired. She stretched out on the bed and within minutes was asleep. According to reports from the *Indiana Daily Student*, her sleep was far from peaceful. From the minute she drifted off, the girl felt cold and utterly alone. She pulled the blankets tighter around her but was unable to stave off the chill.

The girl started to dream. In her dream she found herself in the middle of a forest, surrounded by contorted trees. She couldn't shake the feeling that she was being watched, that someone or something was approaching her from behind. She whirled around and was startled to discover who was drawing near.

The figure was dim at first, but as it came closer, its features took on a clarity that was all too frightening. She recognized, just barely, the shape as Stanley Rice. Rice's flesh was bloodied and shredded; bits and pieces of it were hanging off his body.

The girl found herself paralyzed by fear—unable to move, unable to scream. Only when the figure attacked her, swinging a gleaming silver pick ax at her back, did she rediscover her powers of mobility. She ran and ran, propelled by the sound of the ax whistling through the air. Then she realized that all she had to do to stop Rice was jolt herself back to reality. And so she did.

The girl awoke, breathed a deep sigh of relief and calmed her shaking body. But then she opened her eyes. And her screams began anew. For there, hovering above her head, was the pick ax from her nightmare.

Those in the house who heard the girl's screams immediately ran to the manager's room. They opened the door to find the girl crazed with hysteria. But that was not all. Resting against the wall was a pick ax. Upon seeing that, the members of the fraternity also succumbed to shock—the pick ax had belonged to their house but had been missing for six months.

Now, years after the incident, those who were members of the fraternity at the time wonder whether the events of that fateful afternoon really did take place. Did Stanley Rice rise from the dead and visit the terrified girl? Or was the girl simply dreaming?

No one denies that the pick ax had been missing, and no one's come up with a plausible explanation for its sudden reappearance in the house manager's room. But most do not believe Rice was haunting the building.

Most are convinced the dream was simply a dream, not to be taken seriously.

Yet there are some believers. And though Rice may not have haunted the building, he does haunt the imaginations of these people.

Parker's Ghost

Hanover College's Parker Auditorium seats 750 people. But 751 patrons watch productions there.

Students and employees have reported that one additional spectator shows up even when the house is full. This spectator has been a dedicated follower of the arts for the past 25 years, which is odd, considering he's been dead since 1958.

Established in 1827, Hanover College in Hanover is the oldest private college in Indiana. It sits on 650 acres overlooking the Ohio River and comprises 34 buildings, one of which is the Parker Auditorium. Since its completion in 1947, the Parker Auditorium has been home to the college's theater department. It was named after former college president Albert G. Parker, Jr.

Judith Nagata, a reference librarian at Hanover College, writes that Parker was born in Highland, Maryland but moved to Illinois when he was a teenager. He obtained a bachelor of arts degree at Park College in Missouri, a bachelor of divinity at McCormick Seminary in Illinois and spent some time in China working as a Presbyterian missionary. The University of Chicago granted him a Ph.D., and in the late 1920s he found his way to Hanover.

In the early 20th century, Hanover College, like so many other institutions, was suffering from the ravages of World War I and the Great Depression. Enrolment had dropped and the school was feeling the financial pinch. Upon becoming president in 1929, Parker started a sizable fund-raising campaign and turned things around.

Parker worked at the college until his death in 1958. In honor of his contributions, the institution dedicated the theater department's auditorium to him. But the building may have inherited more than Parker's name. It may also have inherited his spirit. According to Nagata, stories of hauntings in the auditorium started circulating in the 1960s and persist to this day.

A theater graduate of Hanover College believes he has seen Parker's ghost. One night, while performing a show, the actor had a few minutes offstage. He decided to get a drink of water. The theater was configured so that the audience sat not in the auditorium but on risers right on the stage with the main curtain closed, so the student was able to enter the auditorium without being seen.

In the auditorium, the student encountered a middle-aged man sitting quietly in a seat, watching nothing. He thought it strange but continued on his way to the water fountain in the hallway. As he was drinking, he decided to let the man know that the play was taking place behind the main curtain. He returned to the auditorium, but the middle-aged man was nowhere to be found. He had vanished into thin air.

Another time, the same student had a work session scheduled at the theater on a Saturday morning. He was the first one in the building that day; he remembers clearly that he had to use his keys to get in. He was making his way to the scene shop below the stage when he heard a loud scraping sound coming from above, "like someone dragging a couch." He raced up the stairs but was greeted by nothingness. The stage was deserted, as was the auditorium. A quick tour of the building revealed that all the doors were still locked.

The student believes that the middle-aged man he saw in the auditorium during the show was the ghost of Albert Parker and that it was Parker's spirit who raised the ruckus on stage that Saturday morning. He claims the former college president still haunts the auditorium that bears his name.

It's interesting to think that the man who gave so much to Hanover College in his 30 years as president continues to serve the institution, albeit in a completely different capacity.

4
Historically
Haunted

We are the product as well as the producers of history. Our present is ever receding into our past, and we continue to look to our past to inform our futures. Ghosts are artifacts, relics from the past in whom we find both the original and the familiar. Those apparitions hailing from years long past offer us a glimpse into a world that, for most of us, exists only in textbooks and the imagination. The historically haunted allow us to journey backwards through time and experience the extraordinary.

Tuckaway

Tuckaway. This single word conjures up images of celebrity, wealth and the supernatural for the Hoosiers of Indianapolis.

Tuckaway was built by Thomas Perry in 1907. It was designed by Frank Bakemier, a contractor who was greatly influenced by the bungalow style that had gained prominence on the West Coast in 1900. Constructed from red-stained cedar clapboard, the home was deliberately modeled to look like a cottage.

Tuckaway is situated in a park-like setting in what was once a fashionable neighborhood. To get to the house, people must trek down a long walkway that wends its way through the many trees on the property. The dwelling looks as if it's tucked in among those trees, so naturally it's been dubbed Tuckaway.

The property was transferred to George Philip Meier and his wife, Nellie Simmons Meier, in 1912. Over the years, their renovations transformed the quaint home into a reflection of their elaborate tastes and lifestyle. The setting became the perfect backdrop against which to display their collection of art objects brought back from annual trips to Europe.

Even the house's bathrooms were luxurious, modeled after art-deco style, complete with black glass walls, silver wallpaper and diamond-paned, leaded-glass windows. Gilded wallpaper, created by suspending gold dust in the varnish over the wallpaper, reflected light into the main drawing room, resulting in a warm golden glow.

George Meier first came to Indianapolis in 1899 to open up a design salon. Two years later, he relocated his business to L.S. Ayres, the city's premier department store. He became the store's chief designer and buyer in New York and Europe. With his wife's able assistance, he designed many of the dresses worn by the Indianapolis elite.

At a time when most fashion trends originated in New York, Meier was able to create a name for himself in the Midwest. He was best known for his wedding gowns. He worked for Ayres until his death in 1932.

During their time in the city, the Meiers became respected and valued patrons of the arts. Contributions in their name were regularly made to the Indianapolis Arts Association, the Little Theater Society and the Town Hall Club. Their money also supported working actors, dancers and musicians. It was the Meiers who drew internationally known artists to the Midwest.

In the heady times of the 1920s and early 1930s, many musicians, writers and other celebrities passed through Tuckaway's doors at 3128 North Pennsylvania Street. The Meiers' guest list included the likes of Sergei Rachmaninoff, George Gershwin, Walt Disney, Albert Einstein, Rudy Vallee, Mary Pickford, Joan Crawford and Douglas Fairbanks, Jr. Surprisingly, it was Nellie Meier who attracted such a diverse audience.

Stars flocked to see Nellie because she was a palmist, a fortune-teller. She is remembered famously now for her prediction that Carole Lombard, wife of Clark Gable, would die. Lombard had stopped in Indianapolis on January 15, 1942, on the last leg of a bond-selling tour. On January 16, half an hour after refueling in Las Vegas on the way to California, her plane crashed into a mountain.

Visitors sought out Nellie because they were eager for a glimpse into their future, and to this day they continue to frequent Tuckaway even though the clairvoyant and her husband have long since departed this world. They come for the same reasons as before—to see George and Nellie, or at least the ghosts of the famous couple.

Over the past several years, scores of individuals have reported seeing the spirits of George and Nellie walking the halls of Tuckaway, a home that is now a sort of living museum, furnished not only with the same pre-World War II memorabilia of the Meiers, but apparently with the Meiers themselves.

It is said that George likes to stand at the top of the stairs, a distinguished white-haired gentleman in a white suit, and that sometimes his small, oddly dressed wife accompanies him. The heavy front door reportedly opens and closes on its own, footsteps can be heard echoing down the hallways and up the staircase, furniture moves unassisted, lights dim and the stereo volume changes without human intervention. Those who have seen and heard the apparitions, however, feel that the presence in the home is protective and benign.

Kenneth E. Keene, Jr., who bought the home from Nellie's niece Ruth Cannon in 1972, says that the previous owner's ghost has also visited the house. Keene claims that he was mourning Cannon's death when she appeared and spoke to him. She asked him not to grieve, saying it was too much trouble for her to come back and that he would do just fine without her. She promised if he ever needed her help, she would be nearby. Then she winked at him and disappeared.

Keene still lives in Tuckaway. Today the house has the honorable distinction of being part of the National Register of Historic Places. In death, the Meiers have become nearly as famous in Indianapolis as the stars who once frequented their home.

Visitors to the house may not be able to get their palm read by Nellie now, but perhaps they can catch a glimpse of her or George, and their anxieties about the future may somehow be lessened.

Ghosts of Prohibition

It's hard to believe there was a time when having a simple drink was a crime.

The age of Prohibition was an era characterized by gangsters such as John Dillinger and immortalized in movies like *The Untouchables*. It was a period in which speakeasies—wild locales where inhibitions were stripped away by smuggled alcohol—were hugely popular.

McCordsville, a town in Hancock County just outside of Indianapolis, was home to one speakeasy in particular that loomed large in the public eye. The Plantation Club was built in 1917, and two years later, when the Volstead Act became law, developed into the speakeasy of choice. Its boisterous reputation as a casino and roadhouse grew, resting as it did on the rumors that its patrons included Indiana native John Dillinger and famed Chicago mobster Al Capone. It also boasted cabins where customers tired of the drink could be entertained by hostesses.

Today The Plantation Club is home to Casio's Restaurant and Lounge, and while Prohibition is dead, the era is alive and well in Michael and Donni Nickerson's establishment. Nelson Price, a reporter for the *Indianapolis News*, describes Casio's as being decorated with Depression-era ornaments and furnishings ranging from bulletproof cashier's boxes to menu items named "Dillinger's Downfall." And according to Wanda Willis, a folklore writer, the themed restaurant is the setting of two haunting legends involving the murders of young women.

The first legend describes its deceased as a hatcheck girl who loved to trade jabs, both verbal and physical,

Gangster John Dillinger once frequented the haunted speakeasy of Hancock County.

with the speakeasy's many customers. But while she had many fans among the club's patrons, her husband found her behavior difficult to swallow. He asked her to stop; she refused. The husband's frustration finally reached its breaking point, and one night in a fit of anger he shot her in the hatcheck room. For years afterward, her spirit could be seen roaming the speakeasy's casino.

The second legend also describes its victim as a flirt, but in this case seduction was her job. As one of the speakeasy's hostesses, she regularly entertained clients in the many cabins around The Plantation Club. One evening she failed to satisfy a customer to his liking and he chose to express his displeasure by killing her. Her body was found still dressed in her blue gown. "For years," said Willis to Price, "neighbors reported seeing a woman in a blue gown wandering around the grounds."

No one knows if these tales are true; the murders have never been verified. But the legends do provide the perfect backdrop for the Nickersons' restaurant.

Haunted Hollow

Lawlessness is the context for the following dramatic legend about a headless riverman.

In the early 19th century, when the Indiana Territory was founded and settlement was in its infancy, order had yet to be firmly established. Without the steadying arm of the law, a forbidding element was given free rein to flourish. Along the Ohio River, a crucial vein of commerce in the American heartland, river pirates terrorized boats ferrying passengers and goods without fear of reprisal.

Two miles northwest of what is now Mauckport is Haunted Hollow. Loaded with caves and rocks, Haunted Hollow provided a place from which the pirates could strike quickly and then hide themselves from the light of justice. Flatboats were often attacked, their passengers either killed or taken hostage and then stripped of their valuables. It was a profitable practice, requiring only questionable ethics and a distorted sense of morality.

One night a flatboat floated ashore, the boatmen exhausted from a long day of travel. They were eager to eat and then to sleep. Unfortunately, they made landfall in an area particularly troubled by river pirates. As they relaxed over dinner, they remained blissfully unaware of the evil lurking just beyond the shadows cast by their fire.

A band of pirates attracted by the flames had gathered in the darkness, their hearts and souls infected with the sickness of greed. They waited patiently as one by one the weary travelers made their way back to the flatboat to rest. Gradually, the fire died and the land was plunged into the darkness of a moonless night. The only sounds to be heard were those of rushing water and slumbering people. Satisfied, the band crept out from the forests, ready to seize the boat and plunder its goods.

Unfortunately, one particularly exhausted boatman hadn't managed to make his way back to the flatboat. Instead, he'd fallen asleep right where he'd sat eating his dinner. As one of the pirates picked his way across the shore, he failed to notice the slumbering sailor and tripped over him. The boatman awoke startled, and when he realized what was happening, began yelling.

The flatboat was soon buzzing with activity. The boatmen roused themselves from slumber and hurriedly pushed off from shore. The pirates cursed themselves and raced to catch the boat before it reached the deeper waters of the Ohio. They were too slow. They found themselves stranded on shore, their prize drifting away into the night. But they were determined not to have their evening become a complete waste.

The pirates surrounded the stranded boatman, the unfortunate soul who had the bad luck of bearing the full brunt of their rage. They shot and stabbed him repeatedly, and when his body finally lay still, they cut off his head and hurled it into the Ohio. Then they left his body on the shore to rot.

By 1816, Indiana had become the 19th state of the Union. Settlers began moving into the area in earnest and the pirates found their profession subject to the scrutiny of those more scrupulous than themselves. They were forced to move on, to find new areas from which to practice their trade. But while the lawless element may have departed from Haunted Hollow, something was left behind that will forever mark this untamed period in Indiana history.

According to the legend as explained in *Hoosier Hauntings*, settlers walking the riverbanks and hillsides were terrified by what they described as a man with no head who ambled along slowly and deliberately. The settlers swore that if the thing had had a head, its eyes would be scanning the land looking for something—probably the rest of its body. The presence of the headless riverman led people to dub the land Haunted Hollow, and the name has stuck. It is believed that the ghost walks the land still, even two centuries later, forever lamenting the loss of his head.

There is another theory surrounding the origins of the headless riverman. This one claims that in the early 19th century, a man thought the area of Haunted Hollow the perfect place to seek his fortune. He chose poorly, but he couldn't have known. He landed a boat there and within weeks had constructed a cabin of roughly hewn logs carved out of the forests.

During the day the man operated his kiln, heating limestone he quarried to create lime, which he'd then pack onto his boat and take down the river for farmers to use on their soil. At night he sat along the shore of the Ohio, listening to the soothing sound of its rushing waters and basking in the warm satisfaction of a hard day's work.

The man had found his own personal Eden. But fate decreed that he wouldn't remain long in paradise. One afternoon while he readied his boat to ferry his lime down the river, a band of thieves approached him, robbed him and then killed him. His head was cut off and, along with his body, disposed of in the Ohio River.

The headless riverman of Haunted Hollow might very well be the spirit of this man who sought his fortune along the Ohio only to spend eternity rising from his watery grave to seek out his head.

Lights above the Wabash

The Miami Historical Society has in its possession the key to a 75-year-old mystery. Unfortunately, it's a clue that's caused even more confusion, for it stubbornly refuses to give up its secrets.

In 1927, workers stripping gravel in Jacob Rife's gravel pit just south of the Wabash River in Peru were startled to find the skeleton of a man perched in the dirt. Whoever this person was, he'd been forced into a sitting position with his head thrust between his knees and his body crammed into a hole just 28 inches deep.

The man's worn teeth suggested he was middle-aged when he died. The amount of mineral deposits in his bones revealed he had lain there for years. An investigation was launched to determine who he was.

The oldest residents of the city were interviewed to see if they could recall any story or rumor that might contain information leading to the identification of the body. None could. The crime had simply happened too long ago, and people who might have remembered something were probably pushing up daisies themselves.

There were some who wondered whether there had been a cemetery in the area of Jacob Rife's gravel pit. And if there had been, whether there would be records of a burial or a tombstone bearing a name. But there weren't.

After months of questions, investigators were no closer to solving the identity of the unknown corpse than they had been when the body was first discovered. In the end, the only theory they could offer was that the skeletal remains were the lone evidence of a grisly accident or crime from days when the banks of the Wabash were overrun with an unchecked criminal element.

The bones were given to the Miami County Historical Society, which promptly transferred the find to the Miami County Museum, and the case was closed. But within days it was clear that the mystery was not laid to rest.

Witnesses in and around the Wabash River began reporting the presence of strange orbs of light dancing in the air, hovering ever so slightly above the ground. A persistent mist hugged the earth, and screams were said to rent the quiet night along with pleas of a man begging for justice and revenge.

As explained in Hoosier Hauntings, even now people claim that this man haunts the river, his appearance deepening a mystery unearthed so many years ago.

The Blue Hole

No one knows for sure what evil lurks in a bottomless hole in the Wabash River as it wends its way through Vigo County. But many believe it's something lethal, something that drags people helplessly to their deaths, pulling them down from below into a watery grave with a force few are able to resist.

Tom Moulds, who taught folklore at Indiana University, sent me information on this story. The legend began innocuously enough. A swimmer making his way past what was known as the Blue Hole felt a little tug at his legs. He didn't think much of it, reasoning that it was probably just a weak current. But he felt it again, and then again. And each time it was impossible not to notice that whatever it was that was pulling at him was getting stronger.

The swimmer found his legs being dragged under the surface and then released, his body bobbing up and down amidst the waves. Not ready to panic just yet, he stopped swimming and started treading water, trying to see exactly what was going on. For a moment, the river became calm and the air still. Then, without warning, he was dragged beneath the surface, small rolling waves rippling out from where his head went under. He never resurfaced; bubbles appeared and then the water turned calm.

Not long after, other swimmers went missing, and the people living around the Blue Hole began to think that an evil spirit—perhaps a demon—was stalking the innocent. This provided a convenient cover for unspeakable crimes. During Prohibition, speakeasies and brothels sprung up in the area like so many weeds. Anyone unfortunate enough to cross the wrong individual would find himself fitted with anchors of stones or weights and thrown into the Blue Hole, his disappearance fueling the growing rumor of the Blue Hole demon.

As time passed, the spirit allegedly became bolder, creating a massive wave that carried a school bus full of children into the Wabash. There are no newspaper accounts of the horrible event ever happening, but the conspiracy-minded of Vigo County argued that was because authorities unwilling to lend credence to the stories of the Blue Hole demon erased all records of the tragedy.

Finally, in 1971, a group of divers was sent to plumb the depths of the Blue Hole to find out what it was about this particular place that caused so much heartache and speculation. What they found was a hole far from bottomless; in fact, the divers discovered that the hole was only 22 feet deep and inhabited by nothing that suggested a demon.

But even this find was not enough to convince the suspicious and the paranoid. After all, if the demon was able to make bodies disappear and launch waves massive enough to carry away a bus, then surely it would have the ability to make the hole look just 22 feet deep.

Why? To lull the people of Vigo into complacency, of course; to numb their vigilance until it would return and unleash upon them acts the likes of which they could only envision in their worst nightmares.

5
Bridges & Transport

Bridges connect us, allowing us to cross the greatest of spans with the greatest of ease. They open our worlds and broaden our horizons and are symbols of civilization and creation that we hold dear to our hearts. What would New York City be, after all, without the Brooklyn Bridge or San Francisco without the Golden Gate Bridge? It's a question better left unanswered.

While bridges facilitate transport and can, at times, inspire wonder, they can also be the sites for great tragedy and drama. Travel is easy on a bridge, but so too is death: during its construction or after its completion. For its victims, a bridge isn't about crossing from one side to the other. It's about crossing the planes of existence from life into death. Unfortunately, some never quite make it, and instead find themselves roaming the sites of their deaths.

White River Tunnel Light

Carving its way through the side of a hill above the White River in Indiana is a railroad tunnel. The tunnel is 1737 feet long and curves just enough so that even on the sunniest of sunny days it is impossible to see a light at the end. In this case the darkness just might be a good thing.

On some days, the air within the tunnel is muggy, damp and foggy. On others, anyone curious or bold enough to go into the belly of the hill may catch a glimpse of the paranormal, the eerie lights from the lanterns of a spirit compelled to roam the passageway.

When the tunnel was built in 1857, its walls were not lined with any sort of material to keep rocks or other debris from dropping onto the tracks below and derailing any train that should happen by. Because of this, the tracks had to be inspected by watchmen prior to each train's arrival. The watchmen carried two old-style railroad lanterns to light their way and, if the circumstances warranted, to signal an approaching train not to proceed.

Today, legends surround a number of watchmen who were unfortunate enough to have disaster befall them inside the tunnel. These legends have been recounted in Ronald Baker's *Hoosier Folk Legends*. One story has it that a watchman walking the tracks miscalculated the arrival of a train. Realizing that a locomotive was lumbering towards him, he waved his arms, lanterns in hands, hoping the engineer would see him before it was too late. Of course, whether or not the engineer saw him was irrelevant. The train couldn't possibly stop in time, and the man must have realized that fact.

Headless watchmen still walk the tracks of the treacherous White River tunnel.

The watchman began to run, throwing the lanterns down to speed his way. But in the darkness he couldn't see where he was going. Only when the train began to bear down on him, with its headlights illuminating the tunnel, did he see anything.

The race ended, of course. The watchman tripped over a tie, and as he struggled to get up, the wheels of the train ran over his neck, severing his head. From then on, people have claimed to see his spirit walking the tunnel, swinging his lantern in the blackness or waving the lantern with one hand while carrying his head in the other.

Others believe the ghost is actually that of Dixon, a man who was killed inside the tunnel in 1906. At that time a work crew had begun lining the passageway with bricks, eliminating both the need for a watchman and the possibility that one might get mown down by a train. Working amid the humidity and the heat, fighting the dust and the dirt, these laborers spent hours in the company of only each other.

One day when a group of local girls decided to cut through the tunnel as a shortcut to their homes, a few of the men, fed up with their work and the lack of female company, began accosting them. Dixon, seeing the potential for trouble, ran into the tunnel to accompany the girls, to make sure they made it to their homes safely. In doing so he must have raised the ire of more than a few of his coworkers, because just days later, in the middle of the tunnel, Dixon's lifeless body was found. No autopsy was necessary. All could see he'd died from the pick lodged in the back of his head.

Those who have walked near the midpoint of the tunnel, where Dixon's body was found, have claimed to hear footfalls echoing in the passageway, accompanied by lights emanating eerily from the railroad lanterns Dixon carried to his death.

There are also other variations on the story. Some say that two dead watchmen were found hanging along the tunnel walls on spikes. Another watchman reportedly dropped dead at the sight of a vagrant hanging from a beam. And the ghosts of robbers buried in the tunnel are said to haunt the passageway, too.

Or perhaps the spirits are those of Confederate terrorists who were ambushed on the hill above the White River. The screams of those men, who were bludgeoned to death, can supposedly still be heard.

Regardless of the ghostly origins of the mysterious lights, not seeing the light at the end of this particular tunnel might be a good thing.

Free Springs Bridge

Southeast of Sullivan is a little place called Free Springs. Here a stream runs alongside a railroad track, intersected at one point by a narrow gravel road that leads to a bridge crossing the water. The community is small, one of thousands that dot the state. Unlike most other locales, it is peculiarly blessed with its own brand of the supernatural.

The people of Sullivan County believe that the Free Springs Bridge is haunted, visited often by strange noises and headless ghosts. As explained in *Hoosier Folk Legends*, the tale is particularly strong among the area's youth, who often travel to the structure in the dead of night to catch a glimpse of the varied ghosts that are said to call Free Springs home.

The legend is that at one time there was a tramp who always rode in the caboose of a train that rattled its way across the tracks. Whether he was pushed isn't known, but one night the tramp fell out of the caboose. He landed with his head on the tracks, and before he could lift himself off, the train ran right over his neck.

The man's body rolled into the stream and came to rest under the bridge. Strangely, no one ever found his head or perhaps bothered to look for it. His death, like his life, was likely insignificant to those around him. No great pains were taken to identify the body, either. His headless corpse was simply placed in a coffin and buried.

Just days after the coffin was deposited in an unmarked grave, ghost sightings began to circulate their way through the community. It became clear to all that this ghost could not and would not find peace until he found his head.

Out on the bridge, people claimed to see the disturbing sight of a headless man carrying a lantern. The lantern used to illuminate the darkness must have been useless to a ghost with no eyes, but there the man was, walking up and down the tracks where he met his grisly end, swinging a lantern in one hand, searching for his head.

Unfortunately for the tramp's body, it seemed that the head had ideas of its own. Many claimed that on certain nights they saw not the body but the severed head floating in the air, flitting around in search of itself. Maybe the head could have gotten help from another of the ghosts haunting the Free Springs Bridge.

A while back, near the bridge, a boy and his girlfriend were returning home from a date. The car the fellow was driving suddenly careened across the pavement, crashed into a tree and burst into flames.

The boy apparently escaped the carnage, but the girl's body was found amid the smoldering wreckage. It appears he was unable to rescue her. The boy was never seen or heard from again, and all assumed he had left to live a life elsewhere. Any doubts were laid to rest a year later, on the anniversary of the accident.

People passing by the bridge on that particular day reported the startling sound of a voice coming from nowhere. They were shocked to realize that the voice was calling out a name, the name of the girl who'd died in the flaming car accident a year before.

It is said that every year the boy can be heard calling out for his dead girlfriend. Perhaps the boy and the tramp should put their heads together (so to speak) and help each other find their peace.

Haunted Avon Bridge

In some parts of the world, the word Avon evokes images of door-to-door salespeople plying the latest and greatest in cosmetics. In others, it brings to mind William Shakespeare, the bard who was born in Stratford-upon-Avon. But for those in Indiana, the word dredges up associations and memories of a completely different sort—those of a haunted railroad bridge.

Located southwest of Avon in Washington Township, this particular bridge has been standing since 1907. The concrete structure is 50 feet high and has three main arches. Above the main arches is a series of smaller arches separated by passages. The bridge has the look and feel of a Roman aqueduct, and something more besides. In *Hoosier Hauntings,* K.T. MacRorie recounts its history of tragedy and misfortune.

Fate, it seems, has doomed the bridge from the start. Legend has it that during its construction, a man working on the structure accidentally slipped and fell into the wet cement that would serve as the bridge's foundation. Other workers witnessing the accident left him there, perhaps feeling that leaving the poor man in the concrete was easier than pulling him out and saving his life. They decided to hasten the man's death by pouring the rest of the cement in, ignoring the pleas and screams accompanying their decision.

Now any time a train clatters overhead, it is said the man's rest is disturbed and he screams in revolt. And some people claim to have seen his pick protruding from the concrete, frozen forever in time as a sign of his desperate attempt to free himself from his quickly setting tomb.

The tragic history of the Avon Bridge has produced numerous ghosts.

There are more than just spirits of dead workmen roaming the Avon Bridge. There is another tragic story surrounding this locale, and yet another ghost.

Years and years ago, perhaps even a century, a woman was at home, attempting to nurse her sick baby to health. The baby cried and cried, his body curled up in pain. The mother grew frantic when she realized the baby was burning up with a fever and that they had to get to a doctor.

Gathering her strength and determination, the woman wrapped herself and her baby as warmly as possible and set out into the cold and moonless late November night. The quickest way to town was across the Avon Bridge.

Footing on the railroad bridge was uncertain even in the best of conditions. In the darkness, the mother was forced to inch her way forward, making sure to avoid the gaps wide enough to swallow a body whole. She picked her way slowly, carefully, fighting back panic and anxiety.

Suddenly the tracks shuddered. The bridge began to shake with vibrations that the woman knew could only come from a train. Hoping against hope, the mother began to move more quickly, praying that she not see a train, that she remain cloaked in darkness, knowing that any light she encountered would be from a locomotive bearing down upon her.

And then there it was. The whistle of a train pierced the silence. The woman tried to hurry, but her foot caught in one of the ties. With the train almost upon her, she gave one final wrench and freed herself. She leapt to the side, aiming to land on the ground beneath. She touched down safely, but as she fell through the air, her baby slipped from her grasp and tumbled to his death on the hard ground below.

The mother went insane with grief and died a short time later. It is now said that every time the New York Central chugs its way across the Avon Bridge at midnight, you can hear the cries of a mother desperate to save her child.

And if you don't hear the cries of the mother, you might hear those of a young man who joined her as another poor soul who had the misfortune of crossing the Avon Bridge at a most inopportune time. This fellow was at his best girl's house when he realized that he was late and had to get home soon. The only shortcut available to him was over the Avon Bridge.

The man set out, unable to stop smiling as he thought of his lovely lover. He traipsed across the ties giddily until he heard the train whistle and saw his own shadow on the tracks in front of him. Faced with the reality of a train coming down around him, he jumped off the bridge, hoping that he was close enough to the other side to land on the ground as it sloped into the river. Unfortunately, instead of landing safely, he plummeted through nothingness. He screamed and then crashed into the river, his internal organs turning to liquid like the waters that carried his lifeless body downstream.

Now people claim that, should you be near the bridge on a dark night, you can hear a train whistle and seconds later the scream of the lover who leapt. Tragic, to be sure, but if the man had heard the stories of the mother and her baby and the worker in concrete, he might have avoided the bridge altogether as one particularly cursed and wretched.

The Haunted Azalia Bridge

Mothers are meant to be protectors, sheltering their young from the perils and evils of society, yet once in a while that instinct is corrupted. How else can one explain the story of a mom from Azalia who cast her child into the night air, speeding the infant to certain death?

Nobody knows precisely when, but one night when the moon was hidden behind a bank of clouds and the land was pitch black, a baby was thrown from the Azalia Bridge into the creek below. It is said that should you cross that bridge and look over the edge to the waters, you will see the disturbing sight of the ghost of the youngster wrapped in a white blanket, crying out for comfort. If you walk the bridge on a night when the moon is full, you'll run into the spirit of a woman draped in black, looking down and weeping.

And why shouldn't the woman weep? It is her child in the water, after all. Of course, the ultimate irony is that the woman who gave the infant life was the very one to take it away.

Local legend has it that the baby had been conceived out of wedlock. When the people of Azalia discovered the birth of the bastard, they ostracized the young mother. Being abandoned first by her lover and then by the town was more than the girl could bear. For a while she convinced herself that everything would be all right, that life with her child would be good. But as time passed, she began to yearn for adult company.

As the mother pondered her situation, what she needed to do became clearer. If the baby was the cause of her isolation, then getting rid of the baby would solve her problems.

It would be so simple. The girl could just go to the bridge and let gravity take care of the rest. Perhaps in time she would even be able to convince herself that it had been an accident. Or better yet, she could talk the people of Azalia into believing that her child had been abducted. Surely that would garner some sympathy. A desperate measure, to be sure, but desperate times led to desperate measures.

The mother's mind was made up, so under the cover of night, with her baby wrapped in a white blanket, she made her way to the Azalia Bridge. Looking around to make sure she wasn't being observed, she uttered a quick prayer. With her arms outstretched over the edge, the package in them wriggling and crying, she let her child fall. The bough had broken.

Standing there, the young woman rediscovered her humanity. She could not deny the grim truth. She had killed her child. From that day until her death she mourned her loss, dressing only in black and hiding her face behind a veil. On nights when the moon was full, she'd walk back to the bridge, where she would stand and weep.

This story is outlined in *Hoosier Folk Legends*. To this day, it is said her ghost can still be seen standing on the Azalia Bridge, forever retracing the steps she took in her final desperate bid for acceptance.

6
Haunted Cemeteries

Many gravestones are inscribed with the command to "Rest in Peace." But judging by the amount of supernatural activity reported in cemeteries, very few spirits take the words to heart. To walk any cemetery is to walk with history; to walk a haunted one is a different matter altogether. In the haunted cemetery, the past has taken root and flourished, issuing forth a chorus of voices. Lean in and you can hear the fading whispers of the lonely dreamer, the tortured soul or the broken-hearted. These are the voices of the dead, reminding us not to forget them and the lives they might have touched during their brief stay on earth.

Mary Smith

Few can deny their emotions when they hear the sad story of the short life of Mary Smith. Fewer still can resist their imaginations when they're told the woeful tale of her tragic death.

What follows is an incomplete account, as facts have blurred with legend over the years, and historical records were lost when the Vernon, Indiana, courthouse burned to the ground. But the description is enough to affect even the most unfeeling of souls.

Mary and her sister, Gladys, grew up in Vernon. They were siblings, but to the townspeople, blood was all they had in common. When they were young, people began to whisper about them. While they were walking to school, passersby would point at them and mutter. As they were sitting in church, folk would turn their attention away from the sermon and gossip.

You see, Gladys was all right. She was normal. She could talk and laugh and play with the others. Mary, on the other hand, was someone to worry about. She was quiet, sullen and withdrawn.

As the girls grew, the differences between them became more apparent. And the rumors grew more invasive, more damning. Mary's family did its best to protect her from the gossip, but then tragically both parents died, the father first and a short while later the mother.

Gladys and Mary continued to live in the family home. But Gladys found it more and more difficult to keep back the prying eyes and minds of those around them. She did her best, disarming some with her smile and others with

The troubled ghost of Mary Smith haunts a Vernon cemetery.

her charm. But Mary became more withdrawn, and the less the people saw her, the more they spoke about her.

Soon enough all of Vernon was convinced that Mary was a witch. Who knows how the minds of these people worked? Here again human nature proved itself a mystery.

Late one night in 1837, Mary, home alone, was preparing to go to sleep. She'd already changed into her white nightgown and was ready to get under her covers when she realized that she would need more wood for the fire. She opened the door and walked out around the house towards the woodpile. She didn't know she was being watched the entire time.

As she approached the woodpile, Mary was pushed down from behind. She rolled over quickly, and just before she felt his hot, whisky-laden breath on her face, she got a brief look at her attacker.

Mary's eyes flickered with recognition. Lying on top of her was a burly man who had asked her out on a date days earlier. Like all the other girls in town, Mary had refused his overtures. He'd gone blind with rage. Of all the women he knew, how could the witch reject him? The man's anger eventually gave way to a plan, but to execute it he needed to numb himself, so he spent the rest of his time drinking in the local parlor.

When Mary walked out to get more wood that night, she had no idea that she would be viciously attacked and stabbed to death. Of course, her attacker had no idea that she would spend the rest of eternity haunting her burial place.

After her murder, Mary was laid to rest in Baldwin Cemetery. Little was done about the rapist; the townspeople were convinced that Mary, as a witch, probably bewitched the man and thus received what she had deserved.

Five years later a drunk stumbling around the burial ground tripped and fell on her grave. Apparently, the accident prompted Mary's appearance. The boozer could only gasp and stare when Mary's spirit rose from the ground, a specter in white, long hair blowing in the wind, blood trickling down the front of her gown.

Even now, more than a century after Mary's death, it is said that her ghost can be seen sitting on a stump near her grave, weeping for the loss of her life. Anyone who approaches her will be struck by the sense of foreboding and imminent violence hanging in the air. Perhaps this is Mary's attempt to reach beyond her grave and seek justice for one man's brutal act and a city's cruel indifference.

The Lady in Black

Near the edge of the Stepp Cemetery, close to a small grave, is a tree stump. From that stump, a darkly dressed specter is said to feverishly guard the final resting place of her loved one, someone taken from her by the hands of another.

Some say lightning struck a tree and from its remains this crude chair was roughly hewn. Others claim a relative cut the tree down to create a spot from which he or she could pause and reflect. Regardless, over time the stump has become known as the "Warlock Seat" or the "Witch's Throne." And all because of the legend of the lady in black.

The Stepp Cemetery lies deep within the heart of the Morgan-Monroe State Forest. Even on the sunniest days of summer, the graveyard is lit for just a short while. The rest of the time the tombstones find themselves shrouded within the shadows of the cathedral-like stands of hardwoods, light rippling only through the leaves and branches.

The burial ground, 15 miles north of Bloomington and 5 miles southeast of Martinsville, is named for Reuben Stepp. Stepp, originally of North Carolina, made his way to Indiana in the late 19th century and despite the barrenness of the land, purchased property in the township and settled in to raise corn and pigs with his family of nine.

Life at that time was far from idyllic. Whooping cough, dysentery and influenza were prominent, claiming the lives of children from many households clustered in the area. Perhaps it is the mother of one of these unfortunate youngsters who haunts the Stepp Cemetery. Or maybe it's the widow of a man killed during the Civil War.

The apparition reportedly always wears black, which sharply contrasts with her long flowing locks of brilliant white. She's said to be old, even wizened, but far from ugly. Some accounts paint her as heavyset and wearing a black hat with a chain around her leg.

Why the chain? There is speculation that when the husband of the woman in black was killed during the Civil War, she careened into madness and ended up in a mental institution. Sadly, her insanity prevented her from ever visiting her spouse's grave. So in death she returned to the site, making up for all those years of lost time, all those years chained within her padded cell, pinned under the watchful eyes of physicians and attendants who cared nothing for her grief or loss.

Or perhaps the lady in black is watching over her child. In this version of the legend, a family was riding home from church in their wagon. Hidden among the dense forest was a pack of youths. The kids jumped right into the path of the wagon, scaring the horses. The family screamed, the wagon lurched forward and the motion threw the husband and baby from their seats. Tragically, the two did not survive. The mother buried them in the Stepp Cemetery. To this day, no grass grows on the baby's grave, and should anyone leave an item on the barren plot of earth, it will be removed by unseen forces to a place less insulting to the woman who watches over her dead child.

Some believe the lady in black is there to prevent accidents and tragedies of the past. Like the one in which her daughter was killed, decapitated when the car she was riding in sped off the winding roads of the Morgan-Monroe State Forest and crashed into a tree.

This story goes that one evening the girl and her boyfriend decided to park in the forest. Later, they had to rush back so the girl would be home in time for her curfew. They hastened off into the night, desperately trying to get home before midnight. Unfortunately, in their rush they neglected to note how many sharp turns and blind corners dotted the road. The boy lost control of the car and it crashed. The two were buried in the Stepp Cemetery, but the girl's head was never found.

Soon after, the girl's mother died and couples parking in the forest found their privacy unexpectedly and horrifyingly disturbed by the vision of a gnarled old woman, dressed entirely in black, with the battered and bruised head of a young girl hanging from her neck. The mother, it would seem, had risen from the grave, desperate to warn other children about the dangers of speeding along the forest's winding roads.

The stump itself seems tainted with crimes past. Legend states that anyone who sits on it during an evening will die within the year. Stories abound about individuals who have sat on it and have felt the ice-cold grip of some being around their necks. Others say they've heard both the unearthly cries of a woman in anguish and the mournful melody of a lullaby breaking the hushed silence of the cemetery.

The Stepp Cemetery continues to be used by relatives of those already interred in the grounds of the Morgan-Monroe State Forest. And, it would seem, by the lady in black.

Bonds Chapel Cemetery

Indiana legend includes a story that began with a common element of love and jealousy but ended with a distinctly uncommon conclusion. It is the story of the mysteries of Bonds Chapel and the chain and the cross.

A logger was returning home, a smile on his face. His workday had ended unusually early, offering him a brief respite from his backbreaking labor. He was looking forward to surprising his wife by arriving home early and sharing his good fortune with her. He could not know that his luck would be his undoing.

When he walked into his home, his wife was not the only one who was surprised. The logger was shocked to find his wife in the arms of another man. The logger was overcome with anger and rage, and his mind snapped like dry kindling. He grabbed a logger's chain that was hanging nearby and strangled his wife with it. The logger was not charged with any crime. At the time it was, apparently, his right as a cuckolded husband to react so violently. He would not, however, escape unscathed.

Days later, as he worked chaining logs to a wagon, the logger heard a crack. A chain had broken loose and was whipping itself through the air at breakneck speed. The logger didn't have time to react. The chain broke his neck and he died. His body was laid to rest in Bonds Cemetery, a tombstone marking his place.

This is where the legend turns strange. One year after the day on which the logger had killed his wife, the image of a chain link began to take shape on the logger's tombstone. As the years passed, more links appeared, until they formed the shape of the cross, a holy symbol for a distinctly unholy crime. Most surprising of all, the tombstone was changed during these years, as the cemetery resented the unwelcome attention being directed at the infamous stone, yet the links continued to appear. Now, they carry the weight of the curse the logger wrought upon himself.

Legend has it that should you touch the chain, you will die by the chain. Among the stories is one concerning a rider who passed through the chapel one night near the grave. He didn't touch the grave but raced out of the cemetery when a large white form began to rise from the ground. His head was nearly torn off by a logger's chain stretched between two trees. Had he touched the grave, legend claims he surely would have been killed.

Gypsies Cemetery

Crown Point is home to the Gypsies Cemetery, the final resting place of an ostracized people who gained in death what they could not achieve in life.

Located just off Interstate 65 north of Route 2, this small wooded lot dates back to the early 19th century. It originates from a time when individuals who looked different found themselves pushed to the outside of society's circles.

As its name implies, the cemetery was founded by a band of gypsies on a rural stretch of land that is now called Nine Mile. In 1820, these gypsies, because of trouble with the local townspeople, were expelled from the town of Crown Point. Soon after, they fell victim to an outbreak of influenza. The townspeople refused them medical treatment and supplies, and the harsh winter conditions made recovery all the more difficult.

At the end of the winter, when the last of the snows had melted, the townspeople set out to see whether the unwelcome visitors had departed Nine Mile, taking the dreaded epidemic with them. The gypsies had indeed moved on, but they had left their dead behind. The land was marked with burial mounds and makeshift tombstones.

Some say that in doing so, the gypsies, so poorly treated by the townspeople, left a curse on the area. Others dismiss this idea, as the townspeople soon used the cemetery as one of their own.

The question of whether there is a curse in the region does not seem to trouble the local populace. By all accounts, the Gypsies Cemetery has become a popular place, especially at Halloween. Over the last several years, many residents have visited the site, and most of those have reported strange events and happenings.

One story says that should a Bible be brought to the graveyard, the book will start burning. Another states that the bottoms of the pants of people walking over the grounds will turn red, as if the wearer had walked through blood. Less extreme rumors concern strange smells, areas of sudden warmth or chill and glowing orbs of light arcing their way through the night sky.

People walking near the burial ground have also reported a light from a mysterious campfire illuminating the stands of trees and tombstones like some eerie jack-o-lantern. Of course, when these people moved in for a closer look, the light vanished. The same happened for those who drove by in their cars. When the drivers glanced in their rearview mirrors, they saw blue spheres of light following them, but when they stepped out to investigate, not a trace of the spectral illuminations remained.

Whether or not there is a curse from the gypsies who abandoned the graveyard so many years ago is unknown, but there is definitely something unnatural and unusual about the area. Fortunately, the people of Crown Point seem to have embraced rather than rejected their encounters with the supernatural.

Who knows what the gypsies might have to say about this turn of events? They may have been banished in life, but they appear to have gained acceptance in death.

7
Legends
of Indiana

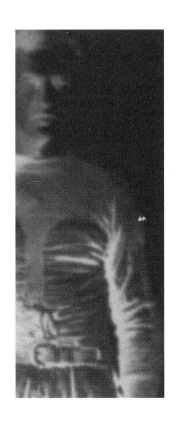

~

Every state has its legends. Like heirlooms, they are passed down from generation to generation, continuing an oral tradition that seems to lose currency with each passing day in our media-saturated culture. There was a time when families might have congregated around the fireplace to tell stories, but today they sit in silence, huddled around a screen. The value of legends cannot be underestimated; their worth is priceless. Legends, like photographs, connect us with our pasts and to times that might exist only in imagination or memory. Sometimes, these stories are all we have to bridge the gap between the past and present.

To listen to their telling is to experience history not recognized or acknowledged by the official record. It is to experience something that transcends our reality.

~

Spook Light Hill

Visitors driving through Indiana are well advised to avoid one particular tourist stop. Unless they're sightseeing for ghosts, that is.

Five miles north of Highway 40 between Terre Haute and Brazil lie three small hills. The second of these is called Spook Light Hill. Get there at the right time, and lights that seemingly come out of nowhere illuminate the area.

A number of legends swirl about these lights like so much mist and fog. All are tragic tales of misfortune. *Hoosier Folk Legends* contains explanations of these legends. Take, for example, the story of a young girl who was heading home one evening when the horses pulling her buggy got startled. The poor girl fell to the ground and the buggy's wheels ran over her neck, severing her head from her body.

The girl's father was worried when his young daughter didn't return home that night, and he put together a search party. Members of the search party found the girl's body the next day. But they could not locate her head. It had mysteriously disappeared.

Just as his daughter's head vanished, so too did the father's sanity. Driven mad by the turn of events and his inability to put his child to rest properly, the man spent the rest of his days combing the hills with his lantern. Though he is now long dead, his light continues to come out every night. Even from beyond the grave, the search, it would seem, carries on.

Another tragic tale surrounding the lights that seem to come out of nowhere also involves a lantern and things lost.

This time, an elderly couple watching their herd of cows come in one evening noticed that one of the animals was missing. They set out to look for the cow and its unborn calf, but try as they might they were not able to find it.

Days after, the two attended a funeral in a nearby cemetery and the old lady fell into the open grave and died. Years later, her husband followed her to the great beyond. Still the lantern lights continued to come out, going back and forth across the hills. Apparently the pair is yet determined to find their cow.

One last legend explaining the mysterious lights of Spook Light Hill has to do with an old man who lived with his daughter on a farm near the area. The farmer was very protective of his daughter. Since the death of his wife years earlier, he had determined that his daughter would never date.

Perhaps the father was afraid of being alone. Perhaps he was anxious about the possibility that his daughter might be swept off her feet and out of his life forever. Ironically, that's not far from what ended up happening to the poor girl.

During the Civil War, a dashing young soldier came to see the farmer's daughter and, tired of being trapped on the dreary farm, the girl begged her father to let her go out with him. Unable to resist her pleas, the farmer finally relented.

The father stood on the porch and watched the pair leave, his heart heavy with sadness. His little girl was growing up. Soon she would depart from his home. It was only natural that she would want to seek out a life of her own, to raise a family as he had. The farmer waited until his daughter disappeared from his sight, then turned and headed back into the house.

The hours passed by ever so slowly. The father sat in his chair, warming his hands and legs by the fire, pausing every now and then to pull out his watch and mark the time. He wondered what his daughter was doing and where she was and hoped that she wouldn't fall in love too quickly and rob him of their precious time together. He thought about his dead wife and cradled a worn photograph of her in his hands. "She's beautiful," he whispered to the picture. "Just like you. I wish you were here to see her."

The farmer smiled as he thought about how eager his daughter had been, how excitedly she'd rummaged through her clothes as she prepared for her night out. And then he frowned, tears welling up in the corners of his eyes, as he remembered how little help he'd been. As much as he loved his daughter, his hard-edged personality and knowledge of farming techniques proved useless when it came to dress patterns and hairstyles.

The father stared at the flames, watching them curl this way and that, casting dancing shadows up onto the walls. Every so often he fed the blaze, until at long last he was down to his last log. As he prepared to throw it into the fire, he paused and drew his pocket watch out.

It was still relatively early for two young lovers out for the night. But for an old man, it was drawing near bedtime. Energy didn't come as easily as it once did, and the cows had to be milked bright and early. The farmer waited until the last of the glowing embers had winked out, then put on his pajamas and climbed into bed. Soon, the sounds of his snoring filled the home.

The farmer awoke the next morning before the sun had even risen, silently cursing the aches in his bones as the chill of the morning air invaded his body. He padded quietly into the kitchen, careful not to wake his child. She was undoubtedly still slumbering peacefully, weary from the night before. He drank a cup of coffee quickly and then, as was his habit, rolled himself a cigarette to smoke on the porch.

When he opened the door, there was no reason for him to suspect anything. Why would he? He had met the soldier, had thought him an upstanding young man. So it was all he could do to keep from falling apart completely. For there, on the porch, was his daughter—dead.

The farmer tried to scream but nothing came out. His hands clasped to his face, his eyes widened with shock. His legs gave way and he stumbled heavily to the ground. He cradled the girl's cold body in his hands, praying, even in the face of the obvious, that she wasn't dead, that she was only asleep.

It wasn't to be, of course. The father buried his daughter next to his wife. Staring across the great expanse of prairie stretching out all around him, the grief of his loss was too much to bear. Something within him snapped with the clap of dry thunder.

The farmer died sometime later, but every night until his death he searched for his daughter's killer, roaming out from his farm to probe the hills for the soldier who had robbed him of his only happiness. People say he is still looking, that the light of Spook Light Hill is that of his lantern as he wanders the land seeking revenge and justice.

Ghost Train

Somewhere in southern Lafayette there was once a tragic train wreck. No one knows the precise location of the disaster, for there are no notable relics. All that has been left as evidence are gruesome ghostly sounds.

On Halloween night in 1864, a 16-car cattle train and an 11-car passenger train collided in the vicinity of 450 South and 450 East, killing many on board. Today it is said that the screech of the two trains straining desperately to slow themselves, and the screams of the dying and injured, remind those close enough to hear how the locomotives couldn't stop in time.

It is also said that the spirits of those killed have yet to find eternal rest. Legend has it that odd lightforms linger over tombstones in a corner of the Greenbush Cemetery, the graveyard that houses the remains of the unfortunate victims.

Matthews Mansion

Sitting at the corner of Maple Grove and Delap in Elletsville, the Matthews Mansion is, by all accounts, a magnificent structure. Unfortunately, the legends that surround the place hint at tragedy and loss. The three-story home has 22-inch-thick limestone walls, 12 rooms and a hand-carved exterior depicting the faces of four of the original owner's 13 children. It is also said to have a curse.

In the early 1860s, just as the country was about to be shaken to its very foundations by the terrors of the Civil War, John Matthews began constructing the dwelling. Working alongside his sons, he quarried limestone with hand drills and blasting powder and used gang saws to cut the gigantic blocks to size.

Progress on the house was halted temporarily when three of Matthews's children were thrown into combat, but the mansion was fully completed by 1867. Despite the opulence of the home, however, it was not a happy place.

One of Matthews's young sons died during Sherman's March to the Sea; a second was killed by shrapnel thrown up by an explosion in the house when a fireplace flue malfunctioned. And the tragedies did not stop there.

Another of Matthews's children—this one extremely young—drew his last breath in the mansion as well. Matthews hung a portrait of his son in memorial. The picture is still there, and nestled between the canvas and the frame is a lock of the boy's hair.

But Matthews may have kept more than the youngster's tuft of hair. Down one particular hallway, a section of wall catches the eye of even the most casual observer.

This segment is thicker than the rest; it looks very much like a closet without a door. Or, if the rumors are to be believed, a tomb without an opening.

It is said that the body of Matthews's young child is buried within that wall, and if not the body of that child, then one of any number of children who lived in the home after the Matthews family departed. Reportedly, the spirit of the youngster still walks the house, trapped, unable to move on. It is sometimes seen lighting a candle on the second story of the home to fend off the darkness.

When it comes to children, the mansion seems to carry a particularly potent and dreadful curse. Two legends involving other families that lived in the house describe young kids dying under the most peculiar circumstances. Both tales hint at a malicious force spiriting away the lives of the children. In the first story, the evil seems supernatural; in the second, it is entirely too grounded in the material world.

One night, a child was lying in his bed, terrified. He was unable to sleep, for he kept hearing sounds. A creak here. A moan there. The inky darkness of his bedroom fuelled his imagination. He ran to his parents' room and woke them up to see if there might be a monster underneath his bed. They came and checked but found nothing of the sort. Reassured, the child climbed back into bed.

The next morning, the parents called out to their son, asking him to come down for breakfast. Strangely, there was no response. They went upstairs to investigate. Instead of seeing their child comfortably asleep, they found his lifeless body. Their house bore no signs of forced entry. All the doors and windows were latched as

The ghosts of children roam the halls of the Matthews Mansion.

they had been the night before, raising the possibility that whoever committed this act was not of this world.

On another night, a different family in the Matthews Mansion prepared for sleep, and a different child heard noises like footsteps and creaking doors all around him. This boy went to wake his parents, too, but his mom and dad remained slumbering, blissfully unaware that someone had invaded their home. The child knew, but what could he possibly do? He was only a little boy, an innocent. Hopefully, he didn't even realize what was happening.

When the parents woke the next morning, they noticed that their house was eerily quiet, too quiet for a home with an energetic child. Before long it became clear why. Their son was dead; he had been killed the night before.

Some believe it is this child that is interred within the house's walls, and that it is his spirit that roams the second floor of the Matthews Mansion with a candle in hand. Apparently he is not alone.

The ghost of Matthews's wife, Mary Ann, has supposedly been seen wandering the home, too. Mary Ann had a habit of pacing the house's roof walk as she waited for her husband to return from work. After he died, she continued with that routine. And today it is said that her figure still walks the roof, unwilling to believe that her loved one is gone.

Throughout the years Mary Ann's spirit has watched her former home go through a variety of reincarnations. Eventually people became too terrified to live in it. Then Indiana University students began using the deserted mansion as a convenient place to party.

In 1955, after 30 years of abandonment, the house was rescued by the city. It was beautifully restored and is now considered a historical landmark. The stories surrounding it have not diminished over time, though. It may well be the case that visitors to the home will encounter much more than they bargained for.

Hammond's Ladies in White

Cline Avenue in Hammond is home to two outrageous legends that deal with women who died tragically on what should have been the happiest days of their lives.

The first of these tales is said to have taken place in 1954. It started when a young man killed his bride and buried her in a graveyard. The man didn't know that the woman was pregnant.

Soon after, townspeople started seeing a lady in white walking the streets of the city. One day, the lady entered a local shop, picked up a bottle of milk and left without paying for it. The next day, she did it again. The third day, the same thing happened, only this time the woman was followed by three men. The trio tracked her to a cemetery, where she disappeared from sight into a grave.

The men looked at each other in bewilderment. It was all they could do to keep their stomachs from lurching. Nevertheless, they gathered up some shovels and began the unenviable task of digging up the grave.

Eventually, the men found the lady. They were stunned to see that she was dead and, judging from both the look and the smell of the body, had been for at least a little while. Covering their mouths with their handkerchiefs, they continued to hollow out the grave. Lying there amidst the dirt were three empty bottles of milk. And next to them, a baby. Most disturbing of all—the baby was alive.

The second legend of a lady who walks Cline Avenue is a tale of ill-fated love. It was told by Mark Marimen in his book *Haunted Indiana*. According to Marimen, Hammond was built upon the backs of immigrant families, most of which came from Poland. These people arrived as the region began to flourish industrially, and they worked the factories in towns such as East Chicago and Whiting. They developed close-knit communities that were insular and isolated.

One of these families had a young daughter named Sophia. As the years passed, Sophia matured and became a beautiful woman with long blonde tresses and deep blue eyes. Naturally, she caught the eyes of many young Polish men looking to settle down and start a family.

The men vied fiercely for Sophia's attention and her parents hoped that eventually she would fall in love with one of them. But none of these young men had a remote chance of capturing Sophia's heart; it already belonged to a 23-year-old fellow from a neighboring community. Sophia had not only fallen in love—she had done so with a Puerto Rican.

From the beginning of their relationship, Sophia and her man recognized that their parents would never support their love. They vowed to keep their affair a secret. For months, they met on the banks of the secluded Calumet River near the outskirts of Hammond. There, bathed in the moonlight and starlight, they shared their hopes and dreams, their desires that one day they could be together forever. There, they decided to find a way to marry.

Although Sophia was uncomfortable with deceiving her family, there was little else she could do. She and her lover managed to persuade a priest in nearby Griffith to marry them without their parents' consents.

Sophia worked for a local grocer and began squirreling away her pay to buy a wedding dress she'd spotted in a store. In late September, the day arrived. Telling her parents that she would be working late and afterwards spending the night at a friend's house, Sophia made her way to the dress shop and bought the gown she'd spent so many nights dreaming about. Then she took a cab to the church, dressed herself in her new dress and sat down to wait for her groom.

Sophia waited. And she waited. And when she finished with that, she waited some more. Her lover never showed up. No one knows why for sure although many have offered explanations. Some say he was rushing to the church when he got into an accident that killed him instantly. Others contend that an accident at the mill where he worked killed him the day before. Still others believe he was just afraid of defying his parents, so he left Whiting, never to return. Regardless, for Sophia the result was the same.

Two hours past the appointed time the priest gently suggested to the young bride that her man was not going to show up. He offered her some tea in his office, but she declined. Instead, she rushed out from the church and into a cab. There, she realized she could never return home. Surely her parents would hear of her plans, and when word spread to the ears of others in the community, she would be ostracized, cast away.

The cabdriver, puzzled as to why his fare was wearing a wedding dress, turned west onto Cline Avenue and approached the Calumet River. At that point Sophia asked him to pull to the side of the road. Then she opened the door and ran towards the water. The driver called after her but she did not heed his call.

Sophia found herself at the exact spot where she had declared her love and planned her marriage. Fueled by desperation and grief, she waded into the river. As she plunged on, the cold waters swept around her. She lost her footing and fell. The current caught at her wedding dress and dragged her ever deeper. Her mouth filled with water, and soon her body drifted lifelessly.

When she did not return home the next morning, Sophia's parents began to search for her. In their beloved daughter's bedroom they found a diary, and reading it, learned of Sophia's intentions. The police were contacted, and two days later the girl's body was identified at the Lake County morgue. Fishermen had found her floating in her wedding dress along the shore.

Sophia was buried in a Hammond cemetery, but her spirit is said to still walk the earth. Motorists passing by the Calumet River on Cline Avenue have reported seeing a beautiful woman in white racing towards the water. Others claim to have ridden with the bride.

One cab driver says he was on his way to Hammond when he was stopped by a young lady. She had long blonde hair and deep blue eyes. The driver was taken by her beauty but was more puzzled that she was wearing a wedding dress in a style that had been popular decades before.

The driver accepted the fare and pulled onto the road. Immediately he felt a chill in the air. He checked his windows and was disturbed that all of them were tightly sealed. What he saw next nearly stopped his heart cold. When the driver looked at his passenger, she was no longer wearing a dress of pristine white but one that was soaking wet and creased with mud.

Panicking, the driver lost control of his cab and swerved across two lanes of traffic. When the vehicle finally stopped, he collected his nerves, took a deep breath and turned to look at his passenger again. He found himself staring at an empty back seat. There was nothing left but the smell of river water lingering in the air.

The Little People

Paul Startzman's search for the little people has been any-thing but short. According to the March 1995 issue of *FATE* magazine, it's been going on for 75 years.

It began one day in 1927, when Startzman was 10 years old and was exploring the paths around the White River in the Mounds State Park in Anderson. He was walking along a trail at the bottom of what was once a gravel pit when he suddenly found himself staring into the eyes of a man who could not have been more than two feet tall.

From where he was standing, Startzman could see that the strange being had dark blond hair and a slightly sun-burned complexion, and that he wore a long, light-blue gown. But that was all he noticed, for the little man, per-haps as surprised and puzzled as Startzman was, turned around and fled down a path that led into a nearby ravine.

When Startzman recovered from his shock, he took to the path in pursuit of the man. To his surprise, the one he followed was nowhere in sight. Before long it became disturbingly apparent that the object of his study had vanished.

Startzman returned to the area again and again, hop-ing to catch another glimpse of the strange being. But he never had any luck until one hot summer day when he and a friend were out hiking and could not shake the dis-tinct feeling that they were being watched.

They kept walking, occasionally glancing behind them. In doing so they saw that they were not alone. Following them was a tiny little man in a long-sleeved gown. They left the woods and entered an expanse of tall grass. They panicked a bit, for the short being continued to trail them.

Eventually the two came to the farmhouse of a friend. They rushed into the home and told everyone present their story. The friend's family was skeptical, but when they looked across the field through a pair of binoculars, all doubt faded. There, atop a great rock along the horizon, was the little man lounging in the midday sun.

Startzman and the others piled into an automobile and drove up the hill. But when they reached the rock on which they had seen the man, the recipient of their interest was gone.

Years passed and Startzman became a scholar of writing, history, archaeology and anthropology. In the course of his studies, he learned about little people common in folklores and mythologies of various cultures around the world. In Ireland, small ones were known as leprechauns. In England, they were called fairies. In Germany, they were referred to as elves.

In America, different Indian tribes had different names for the little people. The Delaware, who lived along the west fork of the White River, called them *Puk-wud-jies*, while the Miamis, who reached as far north as the Wabash, called them *Pa-sa-ki*. Both appellations meant "little wild men of the forest."

In his research Startzman discovered that the little people of America lived in nests and platforms in trees, in miniature huts and teepees that were camouflaged and in caves along the river. To communicate, they tapped on stones with sticks of wood, making sounds similar to those of a woodpecker.

Startzman noted that the little people predated the ancestors of both the Delaware and the Miamis tribes. Their average height was two feet, they wore shirts decorated with bark and grass in the summer, and they donned furs and tall pointed caps in the winter. The older men had beards; the rest were clean-shaven. They moved noiselessly through the woods and were able to disappear with just a single step into a rock, bush or tree.

Startzman became convinced that the little people he had encountered were the same ones spoken about in hushed tones by the Delaware and the Miamis. They had worn a different type of clothing, but that wasn't hard to explain. In Startzman's youth, doors stayed unlocked, clothes dried on lines and every farm had a dump where old clothing was thrown. It would have been easy for anyone to gather the shirts Startzman had seen the little people wearing.

And Startzman wasn't alone in his beliefs. Apparently a friend of his in Muncie was leaving a park after a day of studying when she saw two little men standing in the underbrush watching her. She thought stress was causing her to hallucinate, but when she rubbed her eyes and looked again, they were still there. They stayed for a few minutes, then turned and disappeared.

Startzman has heard of other sightings, too, and he continues to search for evidence verifying the existence of the little people.

Moody Road Lights

In the middle of the day, Francesville's Moody Road looks like an ordinary stretch of highway. But on a clear, still night, it becomes a different place altogether.

Legend has it that motorists driving down the lane after dark will see a strange set of lights in the distance. The lights will bounce above the ground, getting brighter and closer. Then they'll shift to the right or the left and, without any warning, disappear.

If you drive through the area and don't see the lights, there is something you can do to improve your odds. Standing alongside the road is a large tree, the perfect sort of apparatus from which to conduct a hanging. Park under it and blink your headlights three times. Supposedly, the lights will come.

But are you sure you want them to? After all, for the people of Francesville, the lights speak of a horrible legacy.

More than 100 years ago a pioneer farmer lived in the area around Moody Road. He was a headstrong individual, and by most estimations, probably not quite right in the mind. How else could one account for the terrifying way in which he demonstrated his concern for his daughter?

The farmer's daughter had fallen in love with a man her father disapproved of. Despite her father's constant attempts to sever the relationship—which ranged from subtly arranging meetings between his daughter and other eligible young men to attacking her with vicious, ear-splitting tirades—the girl's resolve would not be swayed. She had found her one and only, and nothing, not even her dad, would keep her away from him.

When the farmer realized the full extent of his daughter's devotion, he decided there was only one thing to do. It was terrible, but oh so simple. And the father, believing that he was acting in his daughter's best interests, was able to justify to himself the act he was about to commit.

Days later, the daughter, who had been wondering why her lover hadn't called on her in quite some time, learned the stunning truth. Her own father had brutally murdered the young man who had captured her heart. George Johnson, who once lived near Moody Road, told reporter Alan McPherson of the *Pharos-Tribune* that the Moody Road lights are the ghost of the murdered lover roaming the countryside.

Of course, there are those who are more than willing to offer a scientific explanation for the lights. Moody Road ends at a T-intersection located $2^1/_2$ miles directly south of the end of Highway 49. On cool autumn nights the area is often lost beneath a sea of fog. Some say the lights are actually the taillights of cars traveling north on Highway 49. That the fog surrounding them makes them look as if they're bouncing and shifting.

Either way, the Moody Road lights continue to be a significant part of life in Francesville. Every fall, freshmen at St. Joseph College are initiated to the Moody lights around Halloween, the phenomenon invested with the mysteries of the paranormal. Despite those who offer their scientific explanations for the Moody lights, the lights continue to fascinate because of their basis in legend and folklore.

Diana of the Dunes

In 1915, a woman left behind her family and friends and made her way to the Lake Michigan shoreline in northern Indiana. The shoreline was a wild and desolate place, far removed from civilization, and the few people who did come to the area to swim or fish never ventured far into the dense bordering forests. For someone seeking to escape the past, it was perfect.

No one can say for certain why this woman decided to take refuge amongst the Indiana dunes. Perhaps a broken heart drove her; perhaps she had problems with her family. Regardless, she did not end up finding the privacy she sought.

By summertime, people began to hear stories about the woman who lived as a hermit in the dunes. They came to seek her out, to satisfy their imaginations, to unravel for themselves the shroud of mystery she wore.

The woman spoke little and claimed that she only wanted to be left alone, but the more elusive and timid she was, the more people talked. And the more they talked, the more she became something of a legend. Rumors circulated that the woman was stunningly beautiful and that she wandered the dunes naked as the day she was born. The locals even gave her a name: Diana, a reference to the Roman goddess of the hunt.

Soon the desolate dunes were thronged with the curious hoping to catch a glimpse of the unclothed goddess. Diana shied away from the publicity but, in the end, her home—an abandoned fisherman's shack—was discovered.

"Diana," the elusive denizen of the Lake Michigan dunes

Eventually, a reporter from Chicago managed to wrangle an interview with the misanthrope. What he ascertained flew in the face of all that the people had come to believe about their goddess in the dunes.

Diana, it turned out, was actually Alice Mable Gray, the daughter of a prominent physician. She was an educated woman who had worked for a short while as an editorial secretary for a magazine after her graduation from the University of Chicago. Then, in 1915, she had turned her back on it all and moved to the Indiana

Dunes, a place where she had passed many beautiful days as a child. After stumbling upon the fisherman's shack, she spent her time swimming in the water, exploring the woods around her and reading the books she borrowed from her sojourns into Miller and its public library.

In 1920, Alice met Paul Wilson. According to researcher Mark Marimen, Paul was an unemployed boat builder from LaPorte and by all accounts a far from upstanding citizen. But for whatever reason, Alice fell in love with him and for a while at least, she was happy. The sightseers came less and less frequently once they encountered the commanding physical presence of Paul.

Then, two years later, Paul became the prime suspect in a gruesome murder case. Hikers found the burned body of a man on the beach, and an autopsy revealed that the man had been strangled to death. Paul claimed innocence, and there was not enough evidence to formally charge him with the crime.

Paul and Alice moved to Michigan City to sell handmade furniture and sewing. There, Alice gave birth to two daughters. But while the couple had traded in the rugged lifestyle of the Indiana Dunes for something a little more civilized, their life together was not domesticated. They lived in poverty, and on February 11, 1926, Alice died of what was diagnosed as uremic poisoning, a complication of childbirth. Apparently, massive blows to both her abdomen and back had aggravated her condition. It seems as if Paul Wilson was not exactly the cuddling type.

The lady of the dunes, Alice Mable Gray, was buried in Oak Lawn Cemetery in Gary, Indiana. Today people say she again walks the shoreline she loved so much as a child. Her ghost has reportedly been seen swimming naked in Lake Michigan, and more than one person has claimed to see the spirit of a woman running along the sand only to vanish into the moonlight. Her figure has also been sighted floating near the trees of her old home.

Whether or not the visions are real, Alice continues to loom large in the imaginations of those living around Lake Michigan. In fact, a festival called Diana of the Dunes takes place yearly now. Even in death, Alice Gray is still unable to find the solitude and isolation she so desperately sought in life.

Signs You Shouldn't Ignore

Traveling through the wooded hills of southern Indiana is a good way to escape the pressures of the daily grind. But sometimes it might be better to just stay in and turn on the television.

Something mysterious is said to lurk in the state's southernmost hills. And if the accounts of *Bloomington Herald-Times* reporter Larry Incollingo are to be believed, that something is evil. Legend has it that travelers who hear the flapping of the wings of a giant bird, notice the rattling of a tin cup or catch a glimpse of fox fire are about to lose someone they love.

Long ago, a woman named Julia Hawkins lived a few miles out of Bloomington. By all accounts, she possessed a strange and eerie power: she could heal the sick with just her touch. Julia's ability was known to people everywhere. Some families ventured great distances to bring their ill to her. Others stayed as far away from her as possible.

Those who feared Julia's gift called her a witch. They believed she could see into the future and knew when death was approaching. And supposedly, they were right— Julia did have that special skill. Unfortunately, for her it was more of a curse than a blessing. Julia could not cure all illnesses, and knowing of certain death and being power-less to stop it struck at the very foundations of her being.

The story goes that Julia had a large family and many grandchildren. One day one of her granddaugh-ters became extremely ill. Tragically, the child lived far away and Julia could not cover the distance to see her. A while later, Julia was walking outside when she heard the distinct sound of giant flapping wings. She looked skyward and saw her sick granddaughter flying over her "like an angel." She noted the time. It was four in the afternoon.

The next day, Julia was informed of her granddaughter's death and the eerie circumstances surrounding it. Apparently, the sick child had lapsed into a coma and regained consciousness only once, long enough to tell her mother that she had gone to her grandma's house for a few minutes. She died immediately afterwards, just a little past four in the afternoon.

This was not the only omen Julia received. Another tale describes how one day she noticed a cup in the kitchen water bucket rattling around, as if it had suddenly come alive. The following day, she received word that her daughter had passed away the day before.

Later, Julia asked her son-in-law what her daughter's last words had been. The widower sadly related that his late wife had expressed a desire to drink one more time from her mother's spring. Julia was stunned by this revelation and shocked when she learned that her daughter's death had occurred at the same time as the tin cup had rattled around inside her water bucket.

Southern Indiana practically pulsates with legends such as these. Omens speaking of near and certain death are said to exist in the form of a dog howling at a moonless sky or an owl hooting on a moonlit night. Or, as in the case of this story, in the form of an eerie phosphorescent light.

According to Incollingo, a young couple was heading home after church one evening when they caught sight of fox fire down the road. They changed direction but the fire moved with them. They turned around to retrace their steps but the fire moved in front of them.

Unable to escape, the pair simply shielded their eyes and continued on their way. When they finally arrived home, their fear was replaced by grief and shock, for standing in the doorway was one of their older children, and in her arms was their infant child—dead.

Purple Terror on Stangle

A dilapidated old bridge in southwestern Indiana is the site of many improper burials. And those who are familiar with ghostly legends will undoubtedly recognize that such disrespect for the dead does not bode well for the living.

The elevated structure crosses the Wabash River and is ravaged by time and nature. But in the late 19th and early 20th centuries, it was in tip-top shape. Trains lumbered across it twice a day to ferry passengers and cargo from St. Francesville to Vincennes. When the locomotive was replaced in large part by the automobile, Maurice Stangle bought the route and turned it into a tollway across the state line.

When conflicts for the continent raged, the bridge was the center of much action. The territory around Vincennes teemed with skirmishes as European settlers, eager to test their fortunes in the new lands opening up to the west, frequently encountered American Indian tribes who were not quite willing to relinquish their hold over their ancestral lands.

Many died in these fights along the banks of the Wabash and, as is so often the case, a large number of those who perished did not receive proper burials. Wanda Willis, a folklorist, writes of one particular shaman who fell into the river during a brawl. The shaman's people did their best to salvage his body, but they were powerless to beat back the unrelenting currents of the river.

Because the shaman's body wasn't properly buried, the man's soul was unable to break from the earth and was doomed to remain trapped forever on the corporeal plane. It is not known when his spirit was first spotted, but it is said his ghost is still seen to this day. Legend has it that those walking Stangle's Bridge might encounter the frightening apparition if they happen to peer over the bridge's edge.

First, a purple hand will extend itself from the depths of the Wabash, twisting this way and that, as if begging for assistance. And then a head will bob up, bloated and glowing, its eyes imploring those who gaze upon it to right the wrongs of the past. Reportedly the face of the disembodied head is purple, as if deprived of oxygen. And always it's crying out for release from its watery imprisonment, pleading to be properly buried.

Some believers say the specter invariably shows up. Others insist it is necessary to honk the horn of a stalled car or flash a car's headlights on and off three times in the middle of the bridge if you want the head to appear. But is the head that of the shaman, or does it belong to some other unfortunate soul?

According to information from Vincennes University, one December night in 1906, Catholic priest J.B. Hatter, apparently ill from a few drinks he'd imbibed in Vincennes, fell from a train as it crossed the Wabash. He survived the drop, but his injuries were too great to overcome, and he later passed away.

Others say the head and hand are those of James Johnston, a distinguished soldier of the Revolutionary War. Over 180 years ago, Johnston was buried in a family cemetery overlooking the Wabash. Legend has it he rises now to prevent trespassers from crossing the land he once owned.

The Hatchet Man
and the Scratch at the Door

Indiana University is the location of a particularly disturbing legend involving a spirit trapped on earth, doomed to spend eternity trying to reverse the past.

Years ago, two girls living in the university's McNutt Quad decided not to head home for Thanksgiving. It was a decision they would later regret, for when all was said and done, their lives would be permanently changed. One scarred; the other snuffed out.

At the time, Bloomington was plagued by a series of murders and sex crimes. A depraved criminal dubbed the Hatchet Man was terrorizing the city. Students staying in the dormitories over the holidays were advised not to go out at night and to remain in their rooms with their doors and windows bolted shut.

Unfortunately, the girls got tired of staying inside. Beyond watching television, they could think of little to do to keep themselves entertained. Overwhelming boredom and the stubbornness of youth convinced them that the horrible things that had happened to others wouldn't happen to them, so they headed out for a night on the town.

It's not known where the two girls went, but McNutt isn't far from Bloomington's main drag, Kirkwood Avenue. That particular street, alive with pubs, restaurants and sports bars, would certainly have enlivened their dreary existence. At least for a while.

At one point in the evening one of the girls got tired and decided to head back to her room. She told her friend that she'd see her later and took off, on foot, alone.

The Hatchet Man of Indiana University

As she walked, she became mindful of the warning that had been issued by the school, and she grew nervous.

Before long the girl thought she heard footsteps and heavy breathing behind her. Maybe her imagination was running away with her, or maybe she really was being followed; in any case, she became quite frightened. She began to jog, faster and faster, until her heart pounded and her muscles ached. When she got back to McNutt, she fled into the building and flew up the stairs to her room.

Only when the door was locked did the girl allow herself to relax and catch her breath. Then her thoughts turned to her roommate. She had arrived home safely; would her friend, too? She decided she would wait up until her friend got back to their room.

The girl tried not to doze, but the next thing she knew, it was morning, and the sunlight peeking in from behind her curtains revealed that her worst fear had come true. Her roommate's bed had not been slept in; its covers lay undisturbed, its pillows still fluffed from the day before.

A gnawing sense of dread began to eat away at the girl's resolve, only to explode into sheer horror when she opened her door. Greeting her eyes was a sea of red. Blood—splattered everywhere. And there, at her feet, was her roommate, whose vacant gaze and ghastly pallor confirmed she was dead.

Blood had pooled beneath the roommate's torn body and continued to drip in a sticky stream from her slit throat. Her fingers were worn to the bone and the door bore the marks of a desperate person using the last of her strength to obtain help. The poor girl had tried to wake her roommate by scratching on the wood. Unfortunately, the scratching was not nearly loud enough to interrupt a heavy slumber. So the Hatchet Man had claimed yet another victim.

It is said that to this day, on certain nights, the sound of scratching can be heard in the dormitory. Apparently the spirit of the dead girl is still trying to wake her friend, in the hopes of avoiding her untimely death.

A Dog's Best Friend

One of the most popular and well-documented legends to come out of the Hoosier State is the legend of a bull-dog named Stiffy Green. Stiffy Green is an odd name, to be sure; but then again, Stiffy Green was an odd dog, in life and in death.

Stiffy Green got his name because of the awkward way in which he walked and because, unlike other bulldogs, he had the greenest pair of eyes most people had ever seen. The dog belonged to John Heinl, a man who lived in Terre Haute in the early part of the 20th century. Heinl was old and spent his days walking through town, smoking his pipe and exchanging greetings with people he passed. Stiffy Green was his constant companion.

Sadly, in 1920, Heinl passed away. His death sent ripples of grief through the community, but no one was hit harder by it than Stiffy Green. When Heinl's body was interred in the family crypt in the Highland Lawn Cemetery, the miserable pet, fiercely devoted to his master, had to be forcibly taken away.

Stiffy Green was sent to live with some of Heinl's friends in Terre Haute. But only a week later he went missing. And not surprisingly, he was found sitting at the door of the Heinl mausoleum. The dog was brought back to his new home, but no matter what precautions the owners took, he continued to find a way to escape and run the few miles to the cemetery.

After months of Stiffy Green's repeated flights, his new masters lost patience with the whole affair. They decided to stop fighting the dog and let him be. Clearly,

Stiffy Green, the loyal companion of John Heinl, in life and in death

Stiffy Green wanted to be near Heinl, so that was where he would stay.

Workers on the grounds found their new pet to be unlike any dog they had ever encountered. Stiffy Green refused food and water and sat patiently at the entrance of the tomb for days at a time through all sorts of weather. It was obvious the bulldog wanted to die. And it didn't take long.

Within weeks of moving to the cemetery, Stiffy Green was dead and his body was stuffed and placed in the mausoleum next to the owner he loved. The two were finally reunited. And according to legend, they were as devoted in death as they were in life.

A worker was leaving the cemetery grounds one evening when he heard the bark of a dog, sounding uncannily like Stiffy Green, from the direction of the Heinl crypt. The workman made his way over to the tomb to investigate. He found nothing out of the ordinary, so he turned back to his car. And that was when he saw them.

Off in the distance, along the fence of the Highland Lawn Cemetery, walked an elderly man smoking a pipe. And by his side, barking joyously, trotted a stiff-legged bulldog with brilliant green eyes.

Since that day in October 1921, many people in Terre Haute have glimpsed the spectral figures. It seems that even in the afterlife, the two are inseparable.

Visits from the Dead

Two roads in Indiana, on opposite ends of the state, have one ghostly thing in common. Both are said to be home to the spirit of a woman trapped on this earthbound plane.

One of the roads is a back lane in southern Orange County. It's a decaying stretch of pavement that sees very little traffic. So when a couple of friends driving down it on a dark and stormy Halloween night came across a young woman walking in the middle of it, it's no wonder they were taken by surprise.

Legend has it that the two boys were on their way to a dance in Paoli when they spotted the girl strolling alone in the wind and the rain. They stopped the car and asked her where she was going. Coincidentally, she was going to the same dance they were. The friends offered the young woman a ride. When she got into the car drenched and shivering, one of them handed her his coat.

Soon after, the trio arrived at the dance. They became fast friends and danced the night away, pausing only to have a drink or to sit and talk. When the evening was over, they again piled into the old Ford coupe and headed for home. At the girl's driveway, the boys promised their new friend they'd see her soon. They waited until she entered her house, and then they drove away.

The next day one of the boys realized that he had forgotten to get his coat back from the girl. He and his friend drove to the girl's house and knocked on the door. A woman answered and listened quietly as the boys explained what they were looking for. Afterwards, her face creased with sadness, the woman explained that her daughter wasn't home and hadn't been for quite some time. Her daughter had died five years before.

The boys were shocked. They protested, claiming that the girl couldn't be dead because they had just spent an entire evening dancing and talking with her. The mother shook her head wearily; it wasn't the first time young men had appeared on her doorstep asking for her dead daughter. "No one ever believes me," she said. "But the truth is she is dead. If you want proof, visit the graveyard. You'll find her there."

The boys drove two miles down the road to a Methodist church with a tiny cemetery behind it. They wandered among the graveyard's markers, not at all sure what they were looking for. They still didn't believe the mother; they just didn't think her story was possible.

But then they found it: a tombstone inscribed with the name of the girl they'd found walking along the desolate stretch of road. Any doubts as to whether there might have been another girl buried in that graveyard with the same name were quickly erased by the fact that the coat their new friend had borrowed from one of the boys was draped over the marker. The mother hadn't been lying after all.

Across the state, in Lake County, a second coat draped over a second tombstone is evidence of another spirit that walks an Indiana avenue. This legend involves a young lady who died in a horrible car accident on a northern Indiana back lane known as Reeder Road.

Sometime in 1955, Elizabeth Wilson was riding home from a high school dance with a boy she knew when the weather turned frightful. A thunderstorm tore its way through the county, and flashes of lightning illuminated a landscape in chaos. The driver should have pulled his car to the side of the road and waited for the storm to pass, but he decided that the faster he drove, the sooner they would be home.

Unfortunately, the pavement was slick and the boy lost control of the car. When the car crashed into a tree, the girl was thrown from her seat. The driver could only watch sickeningly as his date hurtled through the driving storm and landed face first in a puddle of rain. The young woman died that night, drowning in less than a foot of water.

Twenty-two years after the accident, a high school boy heading home after a school football game decided to save himself a couple of minutes by taking Reeder Road. As he drove along, savoring his school's victory and bellowing along with the radio, he saw, out of the corner of his eye, a young girl walking down the street. He was puzzled, for while Reeder Road had once been a popular thoroughfare, few people drove it at this time, and still fewer walked it.

The girl was dressed as if she was going to a party, but it'd been years since her clothes were fashionable. As the driver got closer, he could see that even in the afternoon sun she was shivering. When he stopped his car, offered her a ride and she got in, he could see why. The girl was soaked even though it hadn't rained for days. Her teeth were chattering and her shoulders were quivering. The boy offered her his jacket, and she gratefully accepted it.

The driver introduced himself, and the girl smiled and said her name was Elizabeth. When he asked her where she wanted to go, she said home and gave him directions to a house near Reeder. To get there, they would have to drive past Ross Cemetery.

When they approached the cemetery, the girl suddenly asked the boy to stop for a moment. Then, before he could even open the door for her, she bolted from the car and into the cemetery. The driver chased after her, but it seemed that she was too quick for him. She was nowhere to be found. Confused and a little frightened, the boy got back into the car and drove home. It wasn't until later that he realized he had forgotten his jacket.

The next day, the boy returned to the cemetery to look for his coat. It took a while but he finally found it. It was draped across a tombstone that bore the name Elizabeth Wilson. The boy took note of the year of death inscribed on the marker: 1955. He tried to find some possible explanation for what had happened, but standing in front of the tombstone holding his jacket, he instinctively knew there was none. He had been visited by a girl who'd been dead for 22 years.

La Llorona

When Mexican immigrants migrated north to work in the steel mills of Indiana in 1940, they took over an entire neighborhood—including its resident ghost.

The newcomers settled in Cudahey, where they banded together to form a safe harbor for their culture among the foreign wonders of their new country. To that end, they diligently protected their stories. So it was only natural that when they began glimpsing the woman in white, they offered their own interpretation of her origins.

People who had already seen the ghostly lady claimed that she was the spirit of a mother who had passed away in the 1930s. Sometime before her death, the mother had been involved in a tragic car accident. She had survived, but her three children had not. Nor had her sanity.

For years, the mother walked up and down Cline Avenue screaming, pleading to know where her children were and when they would return. Even after she died, motorists reported seeing a woman in white standing by the side of the road, only to disappear into the night air when they offered her a ride.

But to the Mexican community, there was only one explanation for the wailing woman. After all, they had brought to America their language, their culture and their stories. Why not their ghost?

When the residents of Cudahey first saw the spirit, they attributed it to La Llorona, a Mexican woman doomed to forever relive the mistakes of her past. Appropriately enough, La Llorona means the "Crying

One," a definition that perfectly described the waifish apparition with the tear-filled stare.

According to legend, La Llorona's story was one of insecurity, loneliness and desperation. In life, the woman had been a young widow who lived in poverty on the outskirts of Mexico City with her two sons. She did what she could to provide for her children, but her best intentions didn't translate into shelter, clothing and food.

One day, a young nobleman from one of the most powerful families in Mexico noticed the widow—whose beauty could not be hidden by the filth of her hardscrabble existence—as she was scrounging in the city's marketplace. Entranced, he arranged a meeting and had the girl brought to his home.

When the girl entered the nobleman's house, her eyes widened, her jaw dropped and her heart swooned. The building was unlike anything she had ever seen; its opulence found a welcome reception within her soul and provided, for the first time since her husband's death, a glimmer of hope for a better life. Had her prayers been answered?

For a time, it appeared that they had been. She and the nobleman became lovers and the widow found herself falling in love, never realizing that for the nobleman it was just lust that bridged the class divide between them. She was so desperate to rise above her social rank—to give her children a better life and to gorge herself fully upon the supreme wealth she had only sampled—that she allowed herself to be blinded to the truth.

Tragically, the widow confessed her aspirations to her lover one evening, asking him when they would be married. With that one question, she sowed the seed of her downfall, for the nobleman merely laughed at the idea, dismissing the notion as preposterous and impossible. How could he, a man of class and social standing, marry a woman whose children were nothing more than the sons of a common peasant, sons who might challenge the inheritances of any children such a marriage might produce?

Spurned, her dreams faded, the widow returned home. As she stood in the room watching her children sleep, a plan began to form in her mind, a fiendish plot that could only have been borne out of desperation. If all that stood between her and the nobleman were the children, then wouldn't disposing of them solve her problems? She could eliminate them and spend the rest of her days on blissful easy street. The more she thought about it, the more attractive the idea became, until she found herself standing in the bedroom, a knife in hand.

It was over quickly. Before the blood on her hands and white dress was even dry, the young widow set off, making her way back to the nobleman's house. Pointing to the bloodstains, she revealed what she had done, offering proof that he would no longer need to worry about her children. She demanded a marriage now. Nothing would keep them apart any longer. The nobleman was aghast. He refused her proposal and summoned his servants to throw her out of the home.

With nothing left to her, the woman's mind completely cracked. She walked the streets of Mexico City in a daze, still in her bloodstained dress, oblivious to the shocked stares directed towards her from the crowds of people. Days passed, and still she wandered, not knowing where to go or who to talk to. The authorities eventually caught wind of what had happened, but before they could apprehend her and punish her for her crimes, her body was found floating in an immigration ditch near her home.

Gambling everything she had for her happiness, the young widow had lost everything, including her life. Her penance? To wander the streets, forever searching for the children she killed.

Nobody knows for sure whether the story is actually true, but what is certain is that when the community of immigrants first encountered the ghostly woman on Cline Avenue in the 1940s, it seemed that their new home wasn't so foreign after all.

Ghostly Hollow

It's been two centuries since this tale of a headless horse-woman supposedly took place. But still the legend of the rider persists.

On a farm northeast of Wheatland, there lived a man, his wife and their six children, the youngest of whom was named Lucy. From an early age, Lucy was stubborn and obstinate. She could be loving and warm, but more often than not, she possessed a temper as fiery as her long red hair.

Lucy's parents harbored a hope that as their daughter matured, her wild spirit would tame. But the reverse held true. Lucy continued to defy her mom and dad, and with age, her problems with the family only intensified. The situation ate away at her mother and father, who couldn't understand how such a beautiful creature could frustrate them so.

The only time Lucy seemed to be content was when she was riding her horse. Although riding was not an activity most proper young women aspired to master, Lucy loved to feel the wind on her face and her long red hair whipping about behind her. She was most relaxed when astride her mount, and had cultivated a reputation as one of the best riders in the county.

Arguments between Lucy and her father inevitably ended with the dad storming off to his bedroom and the daughter storming out of the house. Lucy would seek refuge in the barn, in the stable of her black stallion, and then she would ride along the trails of Knox County, returning only when morning had broken.

Lucy's parents, relieved when their daughter would finally come home, could not help noticing the marked change that came over Lucy after her nighttime rides. The girl would be calm, not argumentative, and life within the family would be at its most harmonious. There was a true feeling of love among them all.

One Saturday night, Lucy announced to her father that she was going to a party a few miles away. Immediately he raised objections. Traditionally, Saturday night had always been reserved for the family. Lucy became indignant. Within minutes, the two were at each other's throats, their voices raised in righteous anger.

Recognizing his daughter's stubbornness, Lucy's father issued an ultimatum. She could either stay home or go to the party. But if she chose the latter, she could never return home again. Who knew that the farmer was a prophet? Lucy did choose the latter, and she did not return home. But not because of her father's threat.

Headstrong Lucy rode off into the dark and stormy night. She wasn't scared; she had ridden the path for years and knew it well. Unfortunately, while inexperience can breed caution, experience can breed overconfidence, and overconfidence can blind one to danger. Lucy wasn't nearly as careful as she should have been that night.

As she was riding along, Lucy's anger faded and she decided to turn back. She realized that what had passed between her father and herself had to be repaired as soon as possible or the rift would become permanent. She spurred her horse on, racing through the darkness and the rain. But in her hurry, she didn't see a branch hanging over the path. She rode right into it at such speed that she was decapitated.

All the while, Lucy's father sat at home, fuming in his bedroom. He couldn't believe his daughter had left. His threat had been an idle one—he'd only made it because he knew his kids were getting older and there wouldn't be too many more nights for them to spend together—but he still regretted what he'd said. He should have just explained himself.

Lucy's father sighed. There was little he could do at the time to amend the situation. All he could do was wait until morning and talk to his daughter when she returned from her ride, as always, calmer. The thought relaxed him and he smiled. Everything would be just fine.

The next morning, Lucy's family awoke, having no idea what was in store for them. The first inkling of trouble came when they discovered the girl's horse in the stable. The two were practically inseparable, yet Lucy was nowhere to be found. When time passed and she still did not show up, they alerted friends and neighbors and set out to look for her.

It wasn't until late afternoon when a neighbor was walking down a path calling out Lucy's name that the girl's fate was discovered. In the long grasses bordering the trail, the neighbor saw something he couldn't ignore: the sun's light playing about on Lucy's long red hair. And in the middle of the path just ahead was another gruesome sight: Lucy's headless body.

The family collected the body, and Lucy was buried in a small plot on the farm. Her father, however, forever haunted by the threat he had made, never quite recovered from the loss. The threat had been empty, to be sure, but in hindsight, the words he had spoken took on the foreboding of an omen.

Years later, people began to whisper that Lucy had returned from beyond the grave. Folks walking down the path on dark and stormy nights heard, off in the distance, the thundering claps of hooves. And saw, moments later, a horse galloping furiously out of the darkness, spurred on by the jabbing heels of a headless rider.

As the stories became more frequent, the path acquired the name Ghostly Hollow, a nod to the tragic death of red-haired Lucy, who now rode the trail in the afterlife, continually seeking to repair the broken bond between father and child.

Blood on the Mantle

A popular legend involving a test of courage is said to have taken place years ago in northwest Indiana. It's not known if there's any truth to the story, but the tale is trotted out each Halloween to set the mood for a night when the supernatural comes out to play.

One day, two farmers who lived near Valparaiso were embroiled in an argument. It wasn't about anything earth shattering, but men are men, and when a man's courage is called into question, he'll defend it to the end. In this case, the two were discussing a haunted house in the area. One of the farmers claimed he could easily spend a night in the spooky structure; the other found the very idea quite funny.

What started out as small talk over a couple of beers quickly turned into a baiting match. Eventually the two came to the conclusion that the only way to settle the argument was to put the farmer's claim to the test. They made a bet. The farmer would spend a night in the haunted house. If he lasted, he'd win a young heifer. If he chickened out, his friend would get a coveted cow. The men shook hands, finished their drinks and set out for the home.

The farmer made his way into the abandoned house and rolled out a blanket to sleep on. His friend sat in his pickup truck and watched the front door, expecting the farmer to come racing out at any time. At first he laughed to himself, thinking about what a welcome addition a cow would be to his farm. Then he became tired and drifted off to sleep.

The friend hadn't been slumbering long when he was awakened by a bloodcurdling scream from the house. He raced out of his truck, through the front door of the home and into the parlor. There, perched upon the fireplace mantle, he saw the farmer's severed head. The friend felt his stomach lurch, and he fought to maintain some semblance of balance. Then he staggered back to his truck and, quite pointlessly, drove off in search of a doctor.

A short time later, the friend returned to the haunted house and led the doctor into the parlor. He was shocked when he found the fireplace mantle completely undisturbed, covered with a thick coat of dust. And he was utterly surprised when moments later the farmer walked into the room, very much alive and with his head most certainly attached.

Apparently, the farmer's courage had been lacking, and within minutes of entering the home, he had decided to leave. Not wanting to lose the bet, he had sneaked out through the back entrance. He had returned only when he saw his friend race off in his truck to get the doctor.

Confusion reigned. If the farmer hadn't been in the haunted house, who had screamed? And whose head had been on the mantle? At first the friend refused to believe that he hadn't seen it; it was all too real. But in time, for his own peace of mind, he allowed for the possibility that maybe he'd had one too many drinks and he'd imagined the entire incident. Still, he often thought about that dreaded night and wondered what really happened.

The friend might not have known what it was he saw, but many others in the area were certain they had a good idea. Years earlier, a family had lived in the house.

A father, a mother, children—the whole bit. On the surface, the family looked perfect. But behind the façade, tensions were reaching their breaking point. The father tried to keep peace in the household, but eventually he concluded that the best thing to do would be to end it all.

One morning, neighbors passing by the home on their way to work encountered a grisly sight. Human heads were speared onto a number of fence posts. The police were summoned, and when they investigated the house, they discovered that during the night the father had decapitated his entire family, placed some of the heads on the fence and displayed others on the fireplace mantle. Then he'd shot and killed himself.

Since then, people exploring the home have reported seeing heads strewn about, looking as fresh as that fateful night when the father sought to find peace within his family. And they've claimed that the heads disappeared almost as quickly as they showed up. As much as the farmer might tell himself he was hallucinating, it seems clear that he came upon a ghostly reminder of a particularly gruesome crime.

Gravity Hill

It happens all the time. A car breaks down and a long line of people drive by without bothering to stop and lend a hand. But out in Mooresville, according to Internet sources, on a place called Gravity Hill just off State Road 42, there is a woman who, despite all she experienced when her car ran out of gas, is always willing to be of assistance.

Sixty years ago, a little old lady was driving up Gravity Hill when her car suddenly stalled. She managed to ease the vehicle onto the shoulder, where she noticed her fuel gauge was on "empty". But even though she was inconvenienced, the little old lady felt fortunate. There was a gas station right at the top of the hill; she wouldn't have far to go.

Unfortunately, Gravity Hill was more than a little steep. And the little old lady didn't want her car rolling down into oncoming traffic while she was walking to the gas station. Without an emergency brake, she decided to push the car up to safety. For a while, she tried to flag down a passing motorist to give her a hand. But no one would stop. Finally, she felt she had no choice but to push the car up the hill by herself.

The little old lady hadn't gotten far when she realized she simply didn't have the strength for the task. The car was beginning to roll back, and try as she might she was powerless to resist its weight. Her footing was precarious and she stumbled. Before long, the car rolled back on top of her and pinned her to the ground.

Lying there, the old lady again marveled at her luck. She was hurt but not too badly. And she was sure someone would come to her aid. Unfortunately, still no motorists stopped. They just rattled on by, their tires mere inches from her exposed head. The lady continued to call out for help, but to no avail. Then she saw a large truck rumbling its way up the hill.

The truck looked awfully close. Too close. The old lady wriggled and struggled, but she couldn't move. The last thing she saw before closing her eyes to utter a silent prayer were tire treads bearing down upon her.

The truck jerked and the driver frowned. What had he run over? He stopped and got out of his vehicle. Immediately, he realized what had happened. He reached down and felt for the old lady's pulse. She was gone.

Days later, the old lady was buried in a simple ceremony. Shortly after that, rumors started that she had returned from the great beyond. People claimed her ghost was roaming the area around Gravity Hill, and with a mission in mind.

Reportedly, the old lady's return was motivated by her grisly death. No one had stopped to give her a hand, so she was determined that wouldn't happen to anyone else, at least not on Gravity Hill.

Should a motorist find his or her car stalled at the bottom of the hill, all he or she needs to do is put the vehicle in neutral. The ghost of the old lady will take care of the rest. For what the woman lacked in life, she gained in death: the strength necessary to prevent a catastrophe.

Legend has it she's rising above her own fate to stand as a symbol of the very best in humanity.

The Leader of the Pack

Sometime in July 1863, a Confederate soldier named Silas Shimmerhorn abandoned his regiment and fled into a forest in southeastern Indiana. Legend has it he's still there today.

Shimmerhorn had been a member of General John Hunt Morgan's troop, which entered Indiana to raid Union supplies and ran smack dab into the state militia. He left either because he didn't have the heart for continued bloodshed or because he was a native Hoosier and was not willing to raise arms against his home state.

Regardless of his reasons, Shimmerhorn was a Confederate deserter in a Union state and his capture by either side would mean death. So the soldier made his home in the wilderness surrounding Versailles, in a cave now known as Bat Cave. There, he eked out an existence, subsisting on what he could kill with his rapidly dwindling supply of bullets and gunpowder.

When Shimmerhorn had exhausted his firearm stores, he fashioned a crude bow and arrow from saplings. And then he found an even better way to hunt. Shimmerhorn shared his wilderness home with a large pack of wolves that frequented the area around his cave. He endeared himself to these predators by feeding them bits and pieces of animals he managed to kill and then joined them as they raided farmhouses for chickens, cows and pigs.

It wasn't long before farmers in the area started noticing strange wounds on their animals. Beside the telltale signs of wolves' teeth, amidst the blood and the fur, they found cuts that were so precise they could only have been made by a knife. The farmers became wary and alert and started forgoing sleep to stay up nights, training the barrels of their shotguns on their fields.

Soon the farmers began reporting that a man was running wild with a marauding wolf pack. The man wore no shirt or shoes and had long matted hair and beard. Those who managed to catch a glimpse of his eyes swore that they saw straight into the heart of insanity.

The farmers tried to capture the Wolf Man, but he was far too cunning for them. They managed to make their way to his lair, but were greeted by the bared fangs and howls of the wolf pack. They attempted to reason with him, but they just couldn't reach him. His was an untouchable mind.

The Wolf Man continued to raid farmhouses and evade capture, but his days were numbered. Settlers began to arrive in force, and the wolves started disappearing from the area. In time, the stories of the Wolf Man passed into memory, and fact blurred with myth. One group of farmers braved a journey to the Bat Cave, but all they found were the decaying remnants of a pine straw bed and a rifle inscribed with the initials SH. There was no sign of Shimmerhorn.

Years later, farmers suddenly had reason to fear the Wolf Man again. Reportedly, a wolf pack was seen running through a field alongside a barely clothed man with long matted hair, a mangy beard and wild flashing eyes. Allegedly, the wolves—and the man—disappeared into thin air as quickly and mysteriously as they had appeared.

This legend, as written up in *Hoosier Hauntings*, claims that those camping in what has become Versailles State Park are still able to hear the howls of that ghostly wolf pack. And they're still able to catch a glimpse of the phantom hermit who accompanies it.

ENJOY MORE HAUNTING TALES IN THESE COLLECTIONS BY GHOST HOUSE BOOKS

GHOST HOUSE

The colorful history of North America includes many spine-tingling tales of the supernatural. These fun, fascinating books by **GHOST HOUSE BOOKS** reveal the rich diversity of haunted places on the continent.

GHOST STORIES OF AMERICA VOL 1
by Dan Asfar and Edrick Thay
A unique and spine-tingling view of America with stories gathered from all 50 states.
$10.95 US • 5.25" x 8.25" • 248 pages
ISBN-10: 1-894877-11-X • ISBN-13: 978-1-894877-11-4

GHOST STORIES OF OHIO
by Edrick Thay
A collection of tales of ghosts and hauntings throughout Ohio, from Ashtabula and Fairport Harbor to Athens, Columbus and Chillicothe and many places in between.
$11.95 US • 5.25" x 8.25" • 192 pages
ISBN-10: 1-894877-09-8 • ISBN-13: 978-1-894877-09-1

GHOST STORIES OF MICHIGAN
by Dan Asfar
These tales of fright-filled folklore span the length and breadth of the Great Lakes State.
$12.95 • 5.25" x 8.25" • 224 pages
ISBN-10: 1-894877-05-5 • ISBN-13: 978-1-894877-05-3

GHOST STORIES OF MINNESOTA
by Gina Teel
In Minnesota, much more than magnificent scenery will take your breath away. Frightening tales from every corner of the North Star State are sure to chill your spine.
$12.95 • 5.25" x 8.25" • 208 pages
ISBN-10: 1-894877-07-1 • ISBN-13: 978-1-894877-07-7

CAMPFIRE GHOST STORIES VOL 1
by Jo-Anne Christensen
This entertaining collection of great campfire ghost stories, whether read alone or aloud, is sure to raise the hair on the back of your neck.
$12.95 • 5.25" x 8.25" • 224 pages
ISBN-10: 1-894877-02-0 • ISBN-13: 978-1-894877-02-2

These and many more Ghost Stories books are available from your local bookseller or by ordering direct at
1-800-518-3541